BEWARE!!
DO NOT READ THIS
BOOK FROM
BEGINNING TO END!

Making friends in your new town is harder than you thought! The kids in your school are members of the Horror Club. They have their meetings after dark in Bat Wing Hall — a rundown house that's haunted by the ghost of Professor Krupnik!

When the Horror Club decides to play a spooky game, you really want to join in. But then you find out you'll have to search the professor's cursed crypt in the cemetery! Or face an ancient mummy, a witch, and a hungry werewolf — or the terrifying ghost of Professor Krupnik himself — before the night is through!

You're in control of this scary adventure. You decide what will happen. And you decide how terrifying the scares will be.

Start on page 1. Then follow the instructions at the bottom of each page. You make the choices.

If you make the right ones, you'll have a really cool adventure! IF YOU MAKE THE WRONG CHOICES . . . BEWARE!

SO TAKE A DEEP BREATH. CROSS YOUR FINGERS. AND TURN TO PAGE 1 NOW TO *GIVE YOURSELF GOOSEBUMPS!*

READER BEWARE —
YOU CHOOSE THE SCARE!

Look for more
GIVE YOURSELF GOOSEBUMPS adventures
from R. L. STINE

#1 Escape from the Carnival of Horrors
#2 Tick Tock, You're Dead!

R.L. STINE
GIVE YOURSELF
Goosebumps®

TRAPPED IN BAT WING HALL

AN
APPLE
PAPERBACK

SCHOLASTIC INC.
New York Toronto London Auckland Sydney

A PARACHUTE PRESS BOOK

No part of this publication may be reproduced in whole or in part, or stored in a retrieval system, or transmitted in any form or by any means, electronic, mechanical, photocopying, recording, or otherwise, without written permission of the publisher. For information regarding permission, write to Scholastic Inc., 555 Broadway, New York, NY 10012.

ISBN 0-590-56646-6

12 11 10 9 8 7 6 5 4 3   5 6 7 8 9/9 0/0

Printed in the U.S.A.   40

First Scholastic printing, December 1995

"This town stinks!"

It's Friday afternoon — the end of your first week at your new school. Your family just moved to this town last month. And so far no one at school has even tried to be your friend.

Day after day, you sit in class waiting for someone to talk to you. Waiting and staring at all the strange faces around you. How can you possibly go through the year without any friends? you wonder. You're cool. You know you are. You had tons of friends at your old school.

You trudge home slowly. All you have to look forward to is a boring weekend of watching TV with your parents and your bratty little brother. Then something hits the back of your jacket.

You whirl around. A pebble drops onto the ground. You glance up — and notice a brown-haired boy about your own age.

"Hi!" he calls out. "I'm Nick!"

"Hi," you reply and introduce yourself.

"We're in the same class at school," Nick says.

That's funny, you think. You don't remember seeing him there. But you smile anyway. You're so happy someone is finally talking to you.

"I live there," Nick tells you. He points to a two-story green house on the next block. You gaze back at him, shocked.

"But you can't live there!" you exclaim. "There's no way!"

Go on to PAGE 2.

"What do you mean I can't live there?" Nick asks, laughing. "I know my own house."

"I live next door," you tell him. You point to the red-brick house next to the green one. "The green house has been empty all month. There haven't been any lights on. No cars in the driveway."

"I was on vacation with my family. We got back last night," Nick says. "What do you think of school?"

"Okay, I guess," you reply. You're afraid to say anything more. You never know — maybe this kid Nick actually *likes* school.

"Can you believe how much homework our teacher gave us this weekend?" Nick complains. He kicks a stone down the street as you walk. "All the kids who had Mr. McCormick last year say he's really tough. And mean. A total monster!"

You agree. The next thing you know you and Nick are comparing favorite rock groups and comic books. Both of you collect Spider-Man comics. Nick has all the first issues from the last five years, too!

"Comics are cool," Nick says. "But do you know what's even cooler?"

"What?" you ask.

"Horror stories!" Nick exclaims. "In fact, I — " He stops talking and stares at you.

Turn to PAGE 3.

"What?" you ask. "What about horror stories?"

"It's probably way too scary for you," Nick replies.

"Nothing's too scary for me!" you boast.

"That's because you've never been to the Horror Club," Nick says.

"What's that?"

Nick grins. "It's a club I belong to. You've got to be really brave to be a member. When we meet, we tell spooky stories. Really scary!"

"Cool!" you reply. "I love scary stories. Can I join?"

"If you think you can handle it," Nick says. "We meet every Friday night at Bat Wing Hall. That's the deserted house at the dead end of our street. It was old Professor Krupnik's house."

"I've seen the house. It looks haunted," you tell Nick with a laugh.

"Don't laugh," he warns you. "It *is* haunted."

Hurry to PAGE 100.

You crouch over the crack. Your bat sonar tells you that it goes down a long, long way. It might even go on forever. And you're almost afraid to imagine what you might find inside it.

Still, you're a bat.

You're trapped in the crypt.

What have you got to lose?

You take a deep breath to calm yourself. You do a couple of warm-up flaps of your wings. Then, before you can change your mind, you dive head first into the crack. But you're no longer flying!

Instead, you're falling, falling straight down. What are you doing wrong?

In a panic, you check out your wings. To your amazement, they're gone! Those are *arms* flailing around. *Your* arms. You're a kid again!

You don't have time to celebrate. You're falling faster now. And faster. Will you ever land? And will you survive the crash? And if you do, where will you be?

Quick! Turn to PAGE 135.

You want Marcie's help. You swoop around the neighborhood, looking for Marcie's family's name on a mailbox. At last you find it, in front of a small two-story brick house. You peer into all the windows until you find Marcie alone in the living room. She seems to be baby-sitting her little brother, who is about two years old.

You find an open window, then fly into the house. You perch on a curtain in the living room. Below, Marcie and her brother are playing a game with cardboard letters. While you watch, Marcie moves some of the letters.

"C-A-T," Marcie tells her brother. "That spells *cat*, Darryl. Can you say cat?"

"I'm hungry!" the little boy cries.

"I'll get some Jell-O," Marcie says. "See if you can spell cat." She disappears into the hall.

What luck! you think. The letters are small and lightweight! You're sure you'll be able to move them yourself and write out a message to Marcie!

You swoop down to the floor. The letters are in a big box. You start to sort through the letters when Darryl suddenly reaches for you.

"DOGGIE!" he cries. He grabs one of your wings and pulls.

Turn to PAGE 42.

Debbie is standing by herself in the corner. You figure Nick and Connor must still be in the kitchen. You approach cautiously.

"Do you really think this scavenger hunt is for real?" she asks, glancing toward the kitchen.

"Yeah," you say. "You guys *promised* that you'll let me go if I find the items by midnight."

Debbie starts laughing — a hideous cackling laugh. "Fool!" she cries. "It's a joke! You're never going to make it out!"

You don't know whether to believe her or not.

"What do you mean?" you ask.

Debbie slithers closer. "I'm on your side," she whispers. "I used to be a regular kid like you. Then I joined the Horror Club. Now look what's happened to me!"

You stare in amazement at Debbie's hideous monster face. Is she for real? Was she really once a kid like you?

"I want to help you," she says. "If you follow me, I'll help you escape."

If you think Debbie is telling the truth, follow her on PAGE 86.

If you think it's best to continue the hunt, turn to PAGE 16.

"You're on!" Connor growls. "But you go last."
Then he plugs in two more sets of controls.

"Hey, what are you doing?" you cry.

"These are for Nick and Debbie," he replies.

"No fair!" you protest. "I said I'd play against *you*."

"It's all of us or no deal," Connor snarls.

What can you say? You nod and sigh. "Sure. Okay."

"Nick plays first," Connor announces. "And remember — you have to beat *all* of us to win!"

Nick begins to play. You're not too worried, though. You've seen Debbie play. She couldn't even handle level one. How good could Nick be?

Nick makes his first moves. Uh-oh. Nick is excellent.

Connor and Debbie bomb out early. But you and Nick move quickly through the lower levels. Finally, you both reach level twelve — the top level! You've never reached this level before.

Beads of sweat trickle down your face. Up, down, jump! Right, left, shoot! You operate the controls like a pro.

But then the Mud Monsters throw out a tidal wave of mud.

Do you jump the wave or try to duck under it?

Quick! Make a decision! To jump the wave, leap to PAGE 20.
To duck under, slide over to PAGE 72.

"SHAKE!" you instruct the werewolf.

The eleventh chime rings out. *Hurry,* you think. *Hurry!*

The werewolf holds out his paw. Quickly, you pluck three hairs from his forearm.

The final chime never rings. Instead there is an enormous thunderclap. The force shakes the house.

"I did it!" you cry, dancing in a circle. "I got the four items!"

There is no answer.

You gaze around the basement. It's empty. No Nick. No Debbie. No Connor. No werewolf!

"Where is everyone?" you shout. "I won!"

The fire in the furnace has turned to cold ashes. You head for the staircase and climb upstairs.

"Hey, Nick! Debbie? Connor?" you call out.

"In here!" cries a familiar voice. It's Nick!

You race up the steps, two at a time. You follow his voice to the living room of Bat Wing Hall. You feel around in your pocket. You still have the human bone, the mummy's bandage, and the werewolf's hairs. In your other hand, you hold the witch's broom.

You have all the items on the list. The monsters have to let you go — right? You step into the living room.

Turn to PAGE 105.

You step up to the door and grasp the ring in both your hands. It's covered with rust and cobwebs, and you have a feeling it hasn't been moved in a long time.

You pull on it, but the thing won't budge. You clutch the ring even tighter and put all your weight into it.

A hideous screeching noise fills the air. What is making that ghastly sound? Slowly, slowly, the heavy stone door swings open.

Holding your breath, you tiptoe inside. You see a large casket sitting on a stone platform in the middle of the dark room. For a moment, you can't move. You stare at the casket and think: There's a dead person in there. A dead person!

Yikes! Something just grabbed at your hair. You brush it away. And gasp.

A bat flutters off into the darkness, its fangs glinting in the moonlight. Maybe catching a bat isn't such a great idea, you decide.

You quickly search the tomb for scary stuff to bring back to your teammates, but you find nothing except dust and cobwebs. With a final glance, you leave the tomb to rejoin your friends.

There's only one problem. You don't see them anywhere. You're all alone.

Go on to PAGE 93.

You swoop up the stairs as fast as you can. Marcie's right behind you.

You fly into a bedroom. From the crib you know it must be Darryl's room. Next to the crib is a basket containing stuffed animals. There's a stuffed dog, a zebra, a gorilla, a frog, a pussycat, and several stuffed teddy bears.

There's no time to think. Quickly, you flop down into the basket with the other animals. You stay completely still and try to look cute.

A moment later Marcie tears into the room. "Where did that bat go?" she shouts angrily. She stops and gazes all around the room. You hold your breath.

"Hmmph!" she snorts. "It must have gone into my parents' room." She turns and leaves.

You don't waste a moment. Quickly, you fly toward the window. It's open just a crack — but a crack is all you need. You squeeze yourself through the opening and fly into the warm evening breeze.

You're sure you'll have better luck at Lara's house.

At least — you hope you will.

To get to Lara's house, fly to PAGE 118.

"I'm going to search the main floor," you tell the monsters.

"Lots of luck!" Nick sneers.

You glance around the dark creepy mansion. You know escape is going to be tough. You decide you'll do the scavenger hunt. You'll play along with the monsters, but still search for a way out. Either way, you promise yourself, you won't let them turn you into a monster!

You search the living room first. A curtain of cobwebs dangles from the ceiling. You have to part them to search the room. Yuck!

The only furniture in the room is an old sofa and two overstuffed chairs. You lift the cushions to search for the creepy things on the list. Could there really be a human bone under there, you wonder? You nearly choke from the flying dust — but no bone.

You peer under the furniture. Nothing.

Then Connor sneaks up on you. He kicks a dust-ball in your face. "The clock is ticking!" he booms. You stare up at his one bloodshot eye and escape into the next room.

It's an old-fashioned dining room. A long wooden table stands in the middle of the room. As you step toward the table, something black and hairy jumps out at you!

Hurry to PAGE 97.

Could it be a human scream? You've never heard a human scream that sounds like that!

You whirl around in the direction of the scream. Debbie! Debbie is the one screaming.

"NOOOOO!" she shrieks again and hurries over to you.

"Can't you read?" Debbie cries. The warts on her face ooze green goo. "This is not what you want! These aren't *mummy* bandages!" Debbie snatches the bandages from your pockets and tosses them on the floor. "Don't waste time!" she cries.

You step back and try to think. There's no way to escape from the kitchen — Connor is guarding the doors, and Nick is by the window. You *have* to find the items on that list.

You gaze around and then head for a tall, narrow closet.

And freeze in horror.

A thick pool of something red and sticky is seeping underneath the door. It looks like — blood!

What do you do now?

To open the closet door, turn to PAGE 83.

To go back and check the dining room again, go to PAGE 78.

You're sure Nick, Debbie, and Connor are playing a joke on you.

You turn and stare at Nick's reptile-like face. A long, forked tongue darts out at you. You wonder how he does that.

"Excellent costumes, guys," you say. "You really got me."

Connor growls.

"Okay. Enough. Joke's over," you announce. "Take the masks off."

Nobody moves.

You reach over to Nick and grab his face. If he won't take his mask off, you'll do it for him.

The scales feel slippery. You tug and tug.

And then you know.

It isn't a mask.

Nick is a monster!

Too bad you didn't believe him.

Too bad — because with one chomp of Nick's reptile-sharp fangs, you will come to a monstrous

END

Then you hear laughter and footsteps. You jump up from your hiding place and peek out the window. Marcie, Lara, and Martin are standing on the porch. You rush outside.

"Sorry we're late," Marcie tells you. "But we stopped for pizza. Want some?" She holds the pizza box out toward you. Normally triple cheese with extra pepperoni would make your mouth water, but today it smells disgusting. You're more in the mood for moths.

"No thanks," you say. You have no time to lose. "Listen, you've got to come with me to the cemetery." You grab Marcie's arm, but she yanks it back.

"I know I'm acting weird," you explain quickly. "But there's a reason. The other night at the graveyard, something happened. I was transformed — into a bat."

"Right!" Lara cries. "And I became the Bride of Frankenstein."

"It's true," you insist.

Martin snorts. "Great story!" he says, laughing.

"Yeah," Marcie agrees. "Why don't you save it for the next meeting of the Horror Club?"

"It's not a story!" You are practically yelling. In just a few seconds, the sun will go down and you'll never be able to explain!

Go to PAGE 82.

It shouldn't be too hard to make the house seem haunted — especially since it *is* haunted! You turn to the ghost. "I have an idea," you say, "but I need your help."

"You want me to help you?" the ghost booms.

"Yes," you reply and whisper your idea to him.

"All right," the ghost of Professor Krupnik grumbles.

You're very relieved. "Great!" you cry. "And after it works, you'll unbat me."

"We'll see," the ghost mutters. You don't like the sound of that. But you don't have any choice.

You hurry back to the mansion. "We've got to leave!" you tell your friends. "This place is haunted by the ghost of Professor Krupnik!"

"Yeah, sure," says Lara. She yawns.

At that moment the front door to the mansion creaks open. The ghost drifts into the room.

"That's a ghost?" asks Martin. "It just looks like an old man."

"OOOOOOOOOOHHHH!" Professor Krupnik moans. "OOOOOOOHHHH!"

"Even if it *is* a ghost, it doesn't look too scary," Marcie adds. You can't believe it. The Horror Club kids aren't even afraid of a real ghost!

If you try a completely different plan now, go to PAGE 103.

Or if you want to help the ghost scare them away, turn to PAGE 136.

"No offense," you tell Debbie. "But I'm going to continue the scavenger hunt."

For a moment Debbie only stares at you. Then her purple skin begins to grow darker. And darker. "How dare you doubt me!" she cries. "Is this the thanks I get for trying to help?"

She raises her arms. And now you see that she has long — very sharp — claws! She lunges for you.

You leap back, trying to decide which direction to run, when something goes *SPLAT!* — right on your neck.

You reach up and feel prickly hair. And legs. And a warm round body. There's a *tarantula* on your neck!

The creature's legs dig into your skin, like sharp needles. It begins to nibble at your skin. You scream and flick it to the ground. Debbie laughs. She reaches for another deadly spider.

But you spot a dark hall and race down it. Debbie and her tarantulas follow. You run and run. And find yourself standing in front of two doors. One is painted orange. The other is painted green.

Pick a door quickly — before you are eaten alive by the tarantulas!

If you choose the orange door, go to PAGE 126.
If you choose the green door, go to PAGE 43.

"The Horror Club sounds great!" you tell Nick. "Count me in!"

"I'll meet you in front of your house at nine o'clock tonight," Nick says. You agree and say good-bye. Then you rush into your kitchen to find your parents. You tell them you've made a friend, and you've been invited to a club meeting. They're so happy for you. Of course, you don't tell them that the meeting is in a deserted, boarded-up old house!

At nine o'clock, you join Nick under the elm tree in your front yard. A skinny, fidgety girl with messy, long dark hair waits with Nick.

"This is Debbie," he tells you. "She's a member of the club, too."

"Hi," Debbie says. You can barely see her face under all her thick hair. And she always seems to be squirming about! You wonder what's with this strange girl.

You follow your new friends up the hill to the end of the long dark street. The farther you go, the fewer houses there are. At the end of the road, all the streetlights are out. The sky is pitch-black. If it weren't for Nick's flashlight, you'd probably trip over your own feet.

"There it is," Nick says, pointing. "Bat Wing Hall."

Turn to PAGE 96.

ZZZAAANNNGGG! With a loud vibrating noise, the glass box vanishes! The witch stands before you. The magic worked!

"Thank you. Oh, thank you," the witch gushes.

"No problem," you say. "But time is running — "

"You're right," the witch says. "Time's running out." She thrusts her broom into your hands. "Be careful how you remove the straw," she warns.

"Excellent!" you cry. "Now all I have to do is pluck three hairs from a werewolf!"

"Easy!" the witch scoffs. "I know where to find a werewolf."

"You do?" you ask incredulously.

"Sure," the witch says. "The werewolf is in the basement. Or at least he was two hundred years ago. You can take the elevator Professor Krupnik installed." She proudly points to a small elevator in the corner of the attic. Then she disappears in a puff of bright pink smoke.

You hurry to the elevator. The door magically opens. Quickly, you step inside. But the broom gets stuck in the opening!

You frantically try to pull out a straw, but none will come out. You could break one off, you think. But then you remember the witch's warning.

If you take a chance and break off a straw, turn to PAGE 21.

Try to squeeze the broom into the elevator? Then turn to PAGE 115.

"What is it?" you cry, as your body hits the ground.

"We've got to be careful," Nick whispers. "If anyone catches us going in the front door, we could be in big trouble. We're not really allowed in here."

You nod. And watch Debbie as she squirms and glances around nervously.

You wonder why your new friends are so jumpy. You can't imagine how anyone could possibly see you in the darkness. But you figure Nick and Debbie know what they're doing.

You stand and follow Nick and Debbie across the porch. Keeping as quiet as possible, you pull off the broken boards on the front door.

You enter the dark house.

The air in the entryway is stale and dusty. You hold back a sneeze. Nick motions for you to follow him.

You creep after Nick and Debbie down a dark hallway. The floorboards creak loudly with each step.

Then you enter a big, dimly lit living room. A broken chandelier sways from the ceiling. The faded wallpaper hangs in pieces from the walls. Dirty sheets cover what appear to be old sofas and chairs.

And then you see them!

Turn to PAGE 75.

You maneuver your controls quickly and jump over the mud wave.

You made it! Now if you can just destroy the Mud Monsters, you'll win the game.

You concentrate hard. Focus on the screen. You move through snapping turtles and sea monsters. Then, at the right moment, you drop the bombs you saved from level seven.

Boom! You blow up the Mud Monsters' nest.

CONGRATULATIONS! the screen blinks. YOU HAVE DESTROYED THE MUD MONSTERS!

"I win!" you cry.

"I don't believe it!" Nick yells, throwing down his controls.

"How could you lose like that?" Debbie shrieks at Nick.

"How could you let a kid beat you?" Connor snarls. Everyone starts arguing. Debbie and Connor yell at Nick. Nick screams back. They have all forgotten about you.

You decide not to wait around for them to show you out. You're sure you can't trust these monsters. You make a break for the door.

You dodge out into the hall and race down the stairs. Through the downstairs rooms. To the front door. You're almost free!

You grab the doorknob, begin to pull — when someone grabs your shoulder and drags you back!

See who's got you on PAGE 116.

You step out of the elevator. You hold the broom tightly in one hand and choose one straw. Then, with the other hand, you snap it off.

You wait for a moment, standing motionless. Nothing happens. Everything is okay. You breathe a sigh of relief, then stuff the straw in your pocket along with the human bone and the mummy's bandage.

The scavenger hunt is almost over!

You step into the elevator. But — hey, wait! The elevator has vanished!

You plummet through the darkness.

Down, down!

There's no way to stop! You have nothing to help you! In a moment, you'll smash into the basement floor!

Too bad — it seems you made a mistake with the witch's broom. And for you, alas, it's the last straw!

THE END

You decide the best thing would be to tell your friends the truth. You fly outside and as soon as you hit the light, you transform into a kid again. After the movie, your friends rush up to you. "Where were you?" Marcie demands.

"I didn't want to watch the movie," you reply.

"Did it scare you?" Lara teases.

"Afraid of bats?" Martin chimes in. He gives your shoulder a playful punch.

"Actually," you tell him, "the problem is just the opposite. The truth is, I *am* a bat."

All three of your friends stare at you wide-eyed. Then they begin to laugh.

"Right," says Marcie. "And I'm Frankenstein's monster."

"Something happened in the graveyard," you explain. "I was in the crypt, and later that night I turned into a bat."

Marcie and Lara are laughing so hard they can't even talk.

"Wait a minute," Martin says, frowning. "Are you serious?"

"Yes!" you say, relieved that someone finally understands.

But Martin guffaws harder. "What a great story!" he cries.

Go to PAGE 45.

"Maybe there are instructions inside the crypt," you say. You enter, and now you see more writing on the inside of the door. Somehow you never noticed it before:

WARNING: DO NOT USE THE POWER OF THE RING MORE THAN ONCE PER YEAR. RESULTS CAN BE UNPREDICTABLE.

You point out the words to Marcie.

"Oh, no!" she cries. "What can we do now?"

You gaze at your changed friends sadly. Martin seems to be better at flying now, but Lara is having trouble hopping.

"I think we'll have to wait till next year," you tell her.

Marcie hurries across the street to the mansion and returns with an old shoe box. Carefully, you put Lara and Martin into it.

"Don't worry," you say to them. "We'll be able to turn you back in a year. And in the meantime, we'll take very good care of you."

Now all you have to do is figure out how to tell your mother about your strange new pets!

THE END

"Okay," you tell the Egyptian king. "I'll stay."

"Wonderful!" the king exclaims. He steps down from his throne.

"Follow me," he says.

You stick your tongue out at the priest. Then you turn and follow the king from the throne room, down a long hallway and into a small room.

The room has dark marble walls and a low stone ceiling. In the center of the room is a stone table. Your legs begin to tremble when you see what rests on the top — the tray with the strange instruments. The mummy-making instruments!

"Lie down on the table," the king commands you.

"B-but — you said I was going to stay with you!" you protest.

"That's right," the king agrees. "But I am old. I will die soon. And I want to bring you to the afterlife with me. You need to be mummified now!"

The king calls for the priests. They dash in and strap you to the cold table. You kick and yell, but no one pays attention. They are too busy preparing the bandages. *Your* bandages!

One priest holds two instruments over your head. They look like a long, skinny hook and a long, skinny spoon.

"What are you going to do?" you cry.

Go to PAGE 120.

Maybe, you think, the ring has to turn *before* the door is shut.

You're not sure you're strong enough to do it. But you are determined to try.

You swoop down and perch on the rusty ring. Then, while your friends continue to push on the door, you grasp the iron ring in your tiny claws and try to turn it.

At first, nothing happens.

You take a deep breath and try again. Every little bat muscle in you strains. You grunt, you groan. You're shaking all over from the effort.

But at last, the ring starts to turn. And you can feel the door moving inch by tiny inch.

A green mist bubbles out of the tomb. "What's that?" Marcie cries.

"Keep pushing!" you squeak.

Luckily your Horror Club friends don't need any encouragement. They continue to push. With a deafening *CLANK!* the door slams shut.

The ground begins to shake. You hear thunder, and lightning crackles across the sky. An instant later, Lara screams. Your teammates are all staring at you.

Did closing the tomb work?

Turn to PAGE 30.

I can't believe there is a real mummy in this house, you think to yourself as you chase him down hallway after dark hallway.

The mummy turns a corner. You are about to turn, too, when you hear familiar voices behind a pink door. You peek through a crack in the door — and spot Nick, Connor, and Debbie. They seem to be talking about you!

The monsters obviously don't know you are there. Should you stop and listen? Maybe you will hear something that will help you escape.

Or is it better to follow the mummy?

To eavesdrop, turn to PAGE 65.
To follow the mummy, hurry to PAGE 94.

You decide to return to the cemetery tonight. You can't stand to be a bat another second! With a last shuddering look at your new bat self, you climb down from the sink. Then you crawl up the wall to your window ledge. From your new, shorter, bat's-eye view, the yard below looks very far away, even though you're only on the second floor.

Well, you've got wings — might as well try them. You're a little nervous about your lack of flight experience. But you've got no choice. You try flapping your wings, and the next thing you know you're lifting up, up — out into the dark night air.

The wind rushes beneath your wings and you soar higher and higher. You sneak a peek down at the yard far below. Big mistake! For just a moment you're so scared you forget to flap your wings. Instantly, you begin to plummet to the ground.

Frantically, you begin flapping again, and manage to level out. Flying isn't as easy as it looks, you realize. You try to turn to the right, and find yourself flying upside down instead. Then you bump into the side of a tree.

After some practice, you begin to get the hang of flying. Unfortunately, you made so many twists and turns while you were learning that you have no idea where you are.

What now? Go to PAGE 31.

Before you go too far, you feel a strange tingling sensation all over your body. But you don't have time to worry about it. You must escape!

The monsters are gaining on you.

You fly up the stairs now. Two steps at a time. And then you stop. The tingling is getting worse.

Keep going, you say to yourself. You've got to keep going. The monsters are only a few steps behind.

You try to run. But you can't!

Something's wrong. You're stuck in the middle of the staircase! You can't move up. Your legs are paralyzed!

Nick, Debbie, and Connor close in on you. Connor's odor makes you gag. But you're trapped. Frozen in place.

"Need some help?" Nick asks with an evil snicker.

If you accept the monsters' help, go to PAGE 51.

If you refuse, turn to PAGE 61.

You turn to the right. The walls are covered with dirty, dingy wallpaper. It flakes under your fingers as you grope your way through the hall.

You hope you are going in the right direction. But you have no idea where to find a witch's broom — or a werewolf!

Suddenly, you spot a doorway and hear faint beeping noises coming from the room. As you move closer, flashes of light escape the entrance. You enter the room.

Oh, no! There's Nick, Debbie, and Connor!

You're about to run, but then you notice the monsters are sitting around a large screen. Debbie and Connor have controls in their hands. You realize that they are playing a video game!

"Stop, Connor!" Debbie shrieks. "Stop cheating!"

"Shut up!" Connor retorts. "All I have to do is get three apples, and then I can bomb you back to level one!"

You watch in amazement. You recognize the game they're playing — *Mud Monsters*. You can't believe that these three hideous monsters are playing your favorite video game — and playing it badly!

It gives you an idea. The idea is dangerous and very risky — but if it works, it might save your life.

What is your idea? Find out on PAGE 121.

"I don't believe it!" Lara shrieks, pointing at you.

You realize you and Lara are eye-to-eye. That's a promising sign. With your heart pounding, you dare to glance down at your feet. Where only a moment ago, you had claws, now you see your favorite sneakers. Hooray!

You're a kid again!

"We did it!" Marcie cries.

"Welcome back!" Lara says. "What was it like being a bat?"

"How did it happen?" Martin wants to know.

You don't even know where to begin.

Besides, you're sick of the whole thing. You don't want to even think about flying, or eating bugs, or hanging upside down.

"I promise I'll tell you all about it," you tell them. "But not now. It will be my scary story the next time the Horror Club meets."

THE END

There's no sign of your backyard, and you don't recognize any of the houses. And where is the crypt? You don't have a clue.

To make things worse, your bat eyes don't see well enough to help you figure out where you are.

But your ears are a different matter. You were working so hard learning to fly, you didn't pay much attention to your bat hearing. But now you notice that it's excellent.

In fact, it's so good that if you really concentrate, you can get a clear picture of the things making sounds around you.

Off to the right, you hear a big moth flapping its wings. The flapping sounds like soft clapping. Somehow, the sound gives you a complete image of the moth. Below you, the loud humming of a mosquito sounds like a jet taking off.

This is pretty cool!

Now your super-sharp ears hear something more familiar. Something that might help you figure out where you are. You turn toward the sound. You see a man and a woman walking a small dog in the early-morning darkness.

If you ask the couple for help, turn to PAGE 54.

Or if you decide to fly off on your own, soar to PAGE 70.

You've decided to climb into the crypt through the hole. The stone wall looks way too heavy to budge. The crypt is covered with thick carvings, so it's easy to climb up to the top. You push your arms and head into the hole and start to wriggle through.

It's so dark inside, you can't see a thing. As soon as you get your shoulders through, you hear a sound that makes you freeze.

SCRUNK! SCRUNK! It sounds as if something slimy is climbing up the wall toward you. And now you hear another sound — a low moan. There's a moaning *something* climbing your way.

Maybe this wasn't such a good idea.

You try to wriggle back out — but discover you're stuck!

SCRUNK! SCRUNK! The moaning thing is coming closer.

You push and pull. You twist and turn. Nothing. You can't budge.

"Help!" you scream. "Help!" Your voice echoes horribly in the stone room. You begin to kick on the outside of the crypt, hoping your friends will hear you. "Help!"

It's a weird feeling — to be terrified and embarrassed at the same time. You don't know which will be worse — for the moaning thing to get you, or for your friends to come to the crypt and wind up staring right at your rear

END

"Welcome to the Blue Team," Marcie says with a smile.

"Glad you're on the team," Martin adds. He crushes your hand in a hearty handshake.

"So, what are we playing?" you ask.

"The game is called The Hunt," Lara tells you.

"What are we hunting for?" you ask.

Marcie's voice drops down to a croaking whisper. "The creepiest, most terrifying things we can find," she says.

"We vote on which team finds the scariest stuff," Martin explains. "If you haven't chickened out by then, you'll become an official member of the Horror Club."

"Don't worry about me," you say. "I love a good scare."

"Come on," Lara says. "Let's get this game going!"

You follow your teammates outside. Marcie goes first. Her flashlight beam bounces around the overgrown yard, making weird yellow shadows.

You begin scanning the yard, but Martin stops you. "Not here," he says. "You're the newest member. You have to pass the test!"

Test? You don't like the sound of that.

Martin grins and points across the street. "You go there!"

The cemetery!

Turn to PAGE 106.

"I'll take the gray rock," you tell the wizard. You figure the glowing red stone is too obvious — it must be a trick!

He drops the gray rock in your hand. You close your eyes. *Home*, you think. *Take me home.*

You open your eyes. Nothing happens. The wizard lifts an instrument from the tray. It's long and shiny and comes to a razor-sharp point at one end.

"Wait!" you cry. "Wait!"

There's no way anyone is going to make a mummy out of me, you decide. Your eyes dart wildly around the corridor. You spot a small door at the other end. You charge through the circle of priests and barge through the door.

"Oh, wow!" You're standing in a room the size of a football field. Its floors are made of gleaming pink marble. The walls sparkle with real gold, and jeweled lamps hang from the ceiling.

A large throne stands at the far end of the room. And on it sits a very old man with a short gray beard and a crown of golden leaves perched on his head. Surrounding him are a dozen bare-chested men gripping spears.

The old man must be King Ra-ma-la-ma, you realize.

Then you hear the priests' pounding footsteps behind you.

Terrified, you cry out to the king. "Help!"

Will the king help you? Find out on PAGE 52.

The door to the crypt might be your only chance to return home. There's something about this monster you don't trust. Maybe it's the two heads. You need to escape — fast!

"Our history books are over here." The red head points to the opposite wall.

"Geography's on the other side," the blue head booms. It points in the opposite direction. For a moment the monster's arms become tangled, giving you just the time you need.

You dash across the room and yank open the door labeled TO THE CRYPT. Then you throw yourself across the threshold.

And find yourself up to your neck in warm, murky water!

"AROOOOOOOO!" howls a hideous, echoing voice. "WHO HAS COME TO THE CRYPT OF THE SWAMP THING?"

Oh, no! It's the wrong crypt! Looming in the darkness is an enormous creature! It's lumpy and moist, and green slime drips from its arms and legs. Its mouth is lined with sharp, red-tipped teeth. And it's marching straight toward you!

It looks as if this is the end.

But wait!

You have one more chance, if you're brave enough. Turn back now, to PAGE 1. That's right — go back to the very beginning, and join the Horror Club again — if you dare!

THE BEGINNING

You know that Martin lives somewhere in your neighborhood. You fly around reading mailboxes until you find Martin's house.

But your sonar tells you that no one's home. You decide to wait. You flit all around the house, peering in windows. Finally you spot a room with posters from horror movies on the walls. This must be Martin's room. You fly in through an open window and perch upside down on the curtain rod.

Somehow you feel very comfortable with the floor over your head and the ceiling under your feet. You feel so relaxed that you start to doze off.

The next thing you know, something is squeezing you. Hard! You open your eyes. A man with a brown beard has you in his fist, and he's crushing you in his grip.

"Look what we have here!" he says in excitement.

"Be careful, Dad!" cries Martin.

"Don't worry," Martin's father says. "I've got the bat trapped. It can't bite me."

"I'm not a bat! It's me!" you squeak. But they don't understand.

"What are you going to do with it, Dad?" Martin asks.

"There's only one solution," he says, shoving you in a paper bag.

Hurry to PAGE 60.

As the mummy case lid creaks open, you bolt up. Everything looks different. You're not in the upstairs hall of Bat Wing Hall anymore — that's for sure!

You jump out of the case and stare some more. You are standing in a long corridor with walls made of stone. It's cold in here, and you shiver as a chill runs down your spine.

At the end of the corridor you spot a door. You begin to walk toward it when you hear strange voices chanting. The words bounce off the stone walls and echo loudly in your ears.

And then, through the door, a line of black-haired men in long white robes march in. Their eyes seem to cut right through you as they grow nearer. Chanting. Chanting. The same spooky verse over and over again.

"What's going on?" you demand. "Where am I?"

But the men don't answer you. They form a circle around you and slowly move in. Closer.

And closer.

Quick! Go to PAGE 58.

Wrong!

"Tricked you again!" Debbie cries, cackling hideously. "I can't believe you fell for it! Now it's time to turn you into a monster!"

Connor is only inches from you now. You search frantically for a way out.

You tuck your head to your chest. Close your eyes and race back down the hallway — toward Debbie. You barrel right into her and knock her to the ground!

But Nick and Connor are only steps behind.

"Come back!" Debbie wails at you.

You run. Faster. Faster!

Down dark hallways. Footsteps pound behind you.

You have no idea how to get out of this house.

And then you see a door. A bright green door.

Open the door on PAGE 43.

You hold your breath and approach the sleeping mummy. What will happen if you wake it? You move carefully. Inch by inch. You reach your hand out toward the mummy.

SNORRRRF!

You jump back as the mummy lets out a disgusting snore. You pause. Then reach out again.

This time you manage to grab a small piece of bandage that is dangling from its left arm. Quickly, you pull. The bandage rips free, and the mummy didn't even move! What a sleeper!

You have two of the four items on the list, the human bone and the mummy's bandage. Now you only need a straw from a witch's broom and three hairs from a werewolf. But time is ticking.

I've searched the downstairs pretty well, you think to yourself. So the other items must be upstairs.

You spot a narrow, circular staircase behind the mummy case. Up, up, up. Around and around you go. You're getting really dizzy. And the air is ice cold up here. Your teeth begin to chatter. Suddenly the staircase ends in the middle of a musty corridor. You can turn left or right. Which way will you go?

If you are wearing a sweater or a sweatshirt, turn to the right on PAGE 29.

Otherwise, head to the left on PAGE 68.

You stand outside and your skin feels like it's on fire! The sun's glare forces your eyes shut. You duck back inside, wondering what's wrong. Then you try going out again.

The same thing happens. For some reason, you can't stand to be out in the sun! With growing horror, the answer comes to you: You're still a bat!

That's got to be it. You're in human form now, but the transformation must still be in effect. Bats, you remember, sleep during the day. They don't go out in the sun.

You need some time to think.

"I have a headache," you tell your mom. "I'm going back to bed."

"Are you sick?" she asks. She presses her hand against your forehead. "You don't seem to have a fever."

"I'll be all right," you tell her. "I just need to sleep."

You go back to your room. You turn off all the lights and pull down the shades. Then you crawl back into bed and think about your problem. What are you going to do?

And then the answer comes to you!

Go to PAGE 74.

You can't help yourself. You'll never see such a great display of bugs again. Quickly, you lift the lid on the exhibit, grab the biggest beetle, and pop it in your mouth.

"Gross!" Lara screams.

CRUNCH! goes the beetle. Martin and Marcie rush over to the exhibit.

"Watch!" Lara says, pointing to you in horror. You know your friends are staring at you, but you can't stop yourself. You pop beetle after beetle into your mouth. They crunch deliciously between your teeth. You don't stop eating until the police arrive to arrest you for shoplifting rare insects.

You end up in jail. But it isn't that bad — your mom and dad bail you out in less than an hour. And while you hang upside down on the cell bars, you come up with the most amazing idea! An idea that makes you a millionaire!

For days afterward you work in the kitchen — and in the backyard. You chop. You mix. You taste. You add more ingredients and taste again. Perfect!

You have created the biggest craze in ice cream since Rocky Road! You make a fortune with your new flavor — Beetle Berry Crunch.

Ssssh! Please don't give away the secret ingredient — the one that gives it that delicious *crunch*!

THE END

"I'm not a dog!" you squeak at the boy. You pull away. He pulls back. You finally free yourself.

"DOGGIE!" Darryl repeats as he reaches for you again.

"I'm almost through," Marcie calls from the kitchen.

You have to move fast! You grab a clawful of letters and fly to the other side of the room. Darryl starts crawling toward you. Quickly, you arrange the letters in a message:

HELP ME I AM A BAT

You place the last letter just as Darryl reaches you. He grabs at you, but you fly up to the ceiling and perch on the chandelier.

Marcie returns to the living room with a bowl of Jell-O. "Here's something to eat," she tells her brother. Then she notices the message. "Did you do that, Darryl?" she asks in amazement. "I can't believe it! You're a genius!"

"It was me!" you squeak from the ceiling. To let Marcie know who really wrote the message, you swoop down. She takes one look at you and shrieks. Then she grabs a flyswatter from a table and begins swatting at you.

This is no good. Should you give up on Marcie and escape — or try once more to communicate with her?

Escape on PAGE 62.
Or try to communicate on PAGE 123.

You pull open the green door. You find yourself back in the living room. This house is like a never-ending maze, you think.

You glance behind you. No sign of Debbie, Nick, or Connor. You check your watch. It is 10:50 P.M. — you have only a little over an hour before you turn into a monster.

You're trying to decide what to do next when you hear a strange noise.

Thump. Thump. Scrape.

The noise grows louder. And louder.

Thump. Thump. Scrape.

You slowly turn and find yourself staring at a mummy! A six-foot-tall mummy wrapped in old, yellowed bandages that are starting to unravel. Its eyeless, mouthless, bandaged face seems to stare back at you.

A sour smell invades your nostrils. The smell of decay. Of rotting flesh. Of death. You gag and hold your nose.

Then the mummy turns stiffly and disappears down a hallway. You don't want to follow it, but you need mummy bandages for the scavenger hunt. You have to follow it. You have no choice.

Go to PAGE 26.

"Hey, listen, I'm really sorry," you tell the witch. "But I've got to look out for myself now. I'll try to help you later."

Then you grab her broom.

"How dare you abandon me!" the witch shrieks. She starts to mumble a string of weird words. All you can make out is something that sounds like "Amikazoomy!"

At that instant, the handle of the broom glows bright blue in your hand. And then the broom begins to move!

You try to pull away. But you can't!

Your hand is stuck to the broom!

"Hey!" you yell. But it's too late. The broom lifts you up. Higher and higher. You wrap your arms and legs around it and hold on for your life. Then the broom starts to fly!

"Stop!" you yell. You can hear the witch cackling in her box.

You zoom straight to the ceiling. Swerve to the left. Then head for the little window. Faster. Faster!

You crash through the glass!

The icy night air stings your face as you zoom in circles through the sky. You stare down at Bat Wing Hall. Nick, Debbie, and Connor stand on the front lawn, pointing up at you.

You made it out! Too bad now you'll never make it *down* to the ground.

THE END

You realize the truth sounds too batty. Besides, it will be a lot easier to prove what happened if you're already at Bat Wing Hall. You fly outside into the light and instantly transform into a kid again. You wait for the movie to finish, then meet your friends in the lobby.

"Why don't you have a special meeting of the Horror Club, just for the Blue Team?" you suggest. "I never got to tell a story, and I have one that's really scary."

"Good idea," Marcie says. "This mall is boring."

"I have to go home first," Lara announces.

"Me, too," agrees Martin. "We'll meet at Bat Wing Hall in an hour."

It's cloudy, and you're able to ride the bus almost all the way to the mansion. The sunlight only stings a little as you make your way up the hill to the old house.

Your friends better arrive before dark, you think. You know how tough it is to get anyone to listen to you while you're a bat. You glance over at the cemetery and shudder. That's where all your problems began. You breathe a sigh of relief once you've passed it by.

But your relief doesn't last long.

"HALT!" a voice rumbles. You could swear you felt the ground shake. What do you do?

If you halt, turn to PAGE 113.
If you make a run for it, race to PAGE 109.

"I think I know what it's doing," Martin repeats. "It must be practicing flying. It looks kind of cool. I wish I could be a bat."

This is ridiculous.

You're starting to get mad. You fly back across the street again. But this time you keep going. You head straight for the Krupnik Crypt.

"It wants us to follow it!" Lara guesses. Finally! You knew you liked Lara best. She runs after you. The others follow close behind. Soon all four of you are gathered in front of the crypt.

"I wonder why it led us here?" Marcie asks. They all stare at you expectantly.

How can you make them understand that the door needs to be shut? You hover over the dreadful words: WHO TURNS THE STONE WILL GROW BAT BONES.

Marcie watches you, then peers at the words. "Maybe the crypt has something to do with the transformation," she says.

"Yes!" you squeak. "That's it!" But of course they can't understand you. How can you get them to close the door?

Land on the metal ring on the door? Or fly into the crypt?

If you decide to fly into the crypt, soar to PAGE 112.

If you decide to perch on the ring, turn to PAGE 98.

"Okay," you say. "Go ahead."

"You asked for it," Nick says. He glances at Debbie and Connor. They nod with excitement.

What's going on? you wonder.

Slowly Nick brings his hands up to his cheeks. He hooks his thumbs under his chin . . . and rips his face right off!

You gasp. The head of a green-skinned reptilian monster stares out at you from the top of Nick's body. Slimy scales cover his face and begin to spread down his arms and hands!

"N-N-Nick?" you choke out.

The monster grins at you — with six-inch-long fangs! Its beady yellow eyes gaze at you hungrily.

You turn to Debbie and Connor. And scream.

They are peeling off their kid faces, too!

You gape in horror at Debbie. Her skin is now purple and covered with hideous, oozing warts. Her eyes have turned completely white and seem to bulge out of her head. And her hair — it's wriggling with enormous black tarantulas!

Now you know the truth. These kids are monsters!

What next? Go to PAGE 114.

"What game?" you ask Debbie, your voice trembling.

"The scavenger hunt," she declares.

"If you can find all four items on the list before midnight," Nick adds, "then we'll let you go. If you fail, you will be trapped here with us *forever* and turned into a monster. Not much of a choice, huh?"

Your knees shake as you review the scavenger hunt list in your mind. Where will you ever find werewolf hair and mummy bandages? Then again, you don't have many options.

But maybe, you think, you can use the time to search for an open window and escape.

"You've only got two hours," Connor growls, looking at the tiny watch on his huge wrist. "You'd better get started."

"You can begin here on the main floor, or go upstairs," Nick tells you, his reptile tongue darting in and out of his mouth. "It's your choice."

Stay on the main floor, turn to PAGE 11.
Try your luck upstairs, go to PAGE 111.

You're hanging onto the elevator railing by one hand now.

You start to say your prayers, when you hear a strange whooshing sound. A bright blue glow fills the dark airshaft. You glance down. It's the witch's broom, glowing blue, floating up through the air. You bellow with joy!

The next thing you know the magic broom swoops underneath you. Without thinking, you throw your arms around the broom handle.

And you're off!

With a loud *WHOOSH!* the broom flies you down to the basement. What a ride! You leap off the broom, onto solid ground.

You're safe, you think. And then you hear the snarling.

You spin around and spot a furnace belching bright yellow flames. And next to it sits a huge cage — with a pacing, snarling werewolf inside!

Go to PAGE 129.

"I can't believe it! A bat sending me a message!" Marcie exclaims. She beckons to you. "Here, bat. Here, bat. Let me get a better look at you."

Gratefully, you fly over to her. Quick as a cat, she grabs you and shoves you in a drawer.

"Hey!" you squeak. "Let me out of here!"

"This is so cool!" you hear Marcie saying. "A bat that can spell! We can go on TV! We'll be famous!"

"I'm not a bat!" you cry. "I'm a human! Let me finish my message!"

But Marcie isn't interested in your message. "I'll find a box to put it in," she says to herself. Your super bat ears hear her leave the room. A moment later the drawer opens. Darryl's wide eyes stare straight at you.

"DOGGIE!" he cries.

Turn to PAGE 132.

"Yes! Help!" you cry, still frozen in place.

Then you hear Connor's deep, rumbling laughter. "You fell for it! You fell for our trick!" he taunts.

"What trick?" you ask.

"The force field. You're trapped in a force field!" Connor tells you. Debbie and Nick laugh along with him.

"Force field!" you exclaim. "Turn it off! Let me out of here!"

"Sssorry," Nick says with a reptile-like hiss. "You can't escape from Bat Wing Hall!"

"That's right," Debbie sneers. "The force field doesn't turn off until one minute after midnight."

"That's one minute *after* you've turned into a monster!" Connor leers.

Then the monsters lumber down the stairs, leaving you alone. Trapped in the force field. You glance at your watch. Time is ticking away.

You struggle, trying to break through. But you can't budge.

You're stuck.

Stuck until midnight.

Until it's time. Time for a monster of a change!

THE END

Before the king can speak, one of the priests throws his arms around your throat. "Come with me!" he snarls.

"Stop!" the king orders, before the priest can drag you too far. "Who are you?"

"I'm just a kid," you try to explain. "I don't know how I got here. But I really want to go home."

"Let the intruder go!" the king orders the priest. Then he turns to you. "I don't know how to help you return," he admits. "But I like you. And I would be honored if you would agree to stay here with me."

You don't know what to do. Should you stay with the king or leave the palace?

If you accept the king's offer, turn to PAGE 24.
If you decide to leave the palace, sprint to PAGE 89.

You wake up the next morning in your own bed, feeling normal. You scrunch your eyes tight and raise your hands to your face. You're almost afraid to look. You count to three and force your eyes open. Hooray! No more bat wings! Your hands are back! Everything that happened the night before must have been a dream!

A terrible dream.

You rush to the bathroom to examine your face in the mirror. There's no trace of whiskers, or fur, or big bat's ears. You've never been so happy to see your goofy grin! You brush your teeth, comb your hair, and get dressed — whistling the whole time. You skip down the stairs and into the kitchen. The aroma of pancakes cooking fills the room.

"How many pancakes this morning?" your mom asks.

"Three," you tell her. You pour a ton of syrup on the stack and start to eat. But today, the pancakes don't taste good. They're too soft, and the syrup is too sweet. You can't help thinking they'd be better with *beetles* on them.

"I think I'll eat later," you tell your mom. You stand and slip on a jacket. You step outside into the bright sunshine.

And discover you've made the biggest mistake of your life!

Hurry to PAGE 40.

54

You swoop over to the couple. You're just about to ask them for help when the woman notices you.

"A bat!" she shrieks. "A bat! Help!"

Her scream is so loud it scares *you*! You try to fly away. But you still don't have much control. You swoop in the wrong direction — right into her long hair!

You're completely trapped! Your mouth is full of wiry hairs. Hairs wrap themselves around your neck and pull at your claws. You struggle to free yourself, but this only makes it worse.

"AAAAAAACK!" the woman screams.

"Get away!" the man shouts. He grabs for you.

"I'm not really a bat!" you yell. But all that comes out is a squeak.

The woman swats at you — hard! Suddenly you're free. You flutter up, away from the couple. From the top of a streetlight you see a welcome sight — your own house!

You've had enough flying for one night. Wearily, you flutter home. You swoop in through your open window and decide to try again in the morning.

Flip back to PAGE 53.

Once again you're in total darkness.

But at least the crypt door is closed. The stone has been turned. You hope *you've* been turned, too — turned back into a kid.

You wait a few minutes and then stretch out your arms. Your heart sinks. Your fingers are still webbed and still attached to your bat wings. Closing the crypt didn't do anything.

Now you use your bat sonar to examine the inside of the crypt. You notice something you didn't see the last time you were here. There's a crack on the floor of the crypt. You swoop down to investigate. The crack is wide, and deep. It seems to lead straight into the ground. You find these words chiseled along the crack:

WHO ENTERS HERE WILL BE

Will be what? you wonder. Unfortunately, the last part of the writing has crumbled away.

Still, this looks like the same writing you saw on the door of the tomb. Are the missing words TRANSFORMED BACK?

Fly into the crack on PAGE 4.

"Uh, I think that's Martin," you tell Lara and Marcie. The three of you exchange a glance, then stare up at the clumsy bat. There's no doubt about it. Martin turned the ring, so he has been transformed.

"How can we turn him back into a kid?" Marcie asks.

"Maybe if we open the door again," Lara suggests. She reaches for the crypt door.

"No!" you cry. "We don't know what will happen — "

But it's too late. As soon as Lara opens the door she vanishes. But Martin is still a bat!

"Where's Lara?" Marcie cries.

"*RIBBIT!*" You look down at your feet. A small frog is hopping up to you. "*RIBBIT!*"

"I think she's been turned into a frog," you reply.

"This is terrible," Marcie cries. "What can we do?"

Go to PAGE 23.

"Member of the Horror Club, prepare to accept your punishment!" the ghost roars.

"Wait!" you yell, leaping backward. "I've already *been* punished! When I was at the Horror Club Friday night I opened your tomb and was turned into a bat!"

"So that was you!" the professor's ghost exclaims. "Far worse could have happened. But I suppose that's punishment enough."

"But I don't want to be a bat!" you plead. "I want to be a human!"

"Hmmm," the ghost says after a moment. "Perhaps we can help each other. If you will assist me in getting rid of those pesky kids — I'll help you turn back into your true form."

"How do I know you'll do it?" you ask. "Change me back now, and then I'll help you."

"No!" the ghost thunders. "That's my offer. Take it or leave it!"

Can you trust Professor Krupnik's ghost? Should you help him get the Horror Club members out of his house? You don't really have a choice. Besides, he's probably the only one who can unbat you.

To help the ghost and hope he helps you, turn to PAGE 81.

Your heart pounds wildly as the chanting men surround you.

"Halt!" a deep gravelly voice calls out. A tall, white-bearded man dressed in long blue robes has magically appeared behind you. He is holding a clay tray with pots and jars and some creepy instruments you've never seen before.

"Who are you?" you cry. "What's happening?"

"I am the wizard," the man says. "You are in the Palace of Ra-ma-la-ma, an unimportant Egyptian king." He points to the chanting men. "These are the king's priests. And legend decrees that anyone who enters these chambers must be turned into a mummy!"

"A m-mummy?" you cry. "But I came here by accident!"

"No matter," scoffs the wizard. "Prepare to be mummified!"

"Wait!" you plead. You give the wizard your most pathetic look. He takes pity on you.

"I will give you one chance to escape," he declares.

The wizard sets the tray down. He reaches into his robe and pulls out two stones. In his right hand is a glowing red stone. In his left hand is a dull gray rock. "One stone is an enchanted stone," he explains. "It will return you to where you came from. The other stone is an ordinary rock. Pick one."

If you choose the red stone, turn to PAGE 84.
If you prefer the gray rock, turn to PAGE 34.

You decide to cross the river. Just beyond the sign, you notice a rowboat, almost hidden in the mist.

"Want a ride?" asks a deep voice.

You can just make out a figure in a dark cloak sitting at the oars of the boat.

Your skin crawls at the sight of him. His face is skull-like, the bones jutting out like a skeleton's. The last thing you want to do is get any closer to this evil-looking creature, but you have no choice. You have to return to the crypt. You step into the rowboat. Without another word, the oarsman begins to row. You shiver as the boat makes its silent way across the murky river. Finally, the boat docks on the other side and you climb out.

You want to ask directions but the oarsman is already turning the boat around. "Hey," you call out, and wave to get his attention. To your horror, you can see right through your hand.

You turn back around and are relieved to spot the Krupnik Crypt just ahead. You make your way to the entrance and notice the list of the dead people buried there.

The last name on the list looks as if it has just been carved. You lean in to read it and gasp! There on the stone, in undeniable lettering, is your own name . . . and just two more words . . .

THE END

You flap your wings frantically, trying to escape the paper bag. It's no use — you're trapped!

You feel the bag being lifted and carried through the house, down the stairs, and outside into the cool night air. You hear the slam of a door, then the rumble of an engine. You're in a car! But where are you going?

About ten minutes later, the car screeches to a stop. You are picked up and carried across a winding footpath.

"Here we are!" Martin's dad announces.

"Thank you so much," a strange, deep voice replies. "It is always wise to bring lost wild animals to the zoo. We can protect them here. This bat will be much happier with all the other bats in the Bat House."

Bat House? Zoo? Is this guy serious? you wonder.

Suddenly, the bag opens wide and you are nudged out. You flap your wings, confused and disoriented. Then you hear a cage door click shut.

And the flutter of hundreds of bat wings!

There are bats — *everywhere!* Swarming around you, swooping down on you. You head for a corner, terrified. A large bat zooms over and brushes up against you. You try to blend into the wall, but the bat moves closer and closer.

Too bad. It looks as if this bat is *batty* over you!

THE END

"Get away," you cry out to the monsters. "I don't need your help."

The three monsters laugh and laugh.

You try to ignore them. And concentrate on moving.

"He doesn't get it," you hear Nick whisper to Debbie. "He doesn't know he's trapped in a force field."

A force field? Oh, no!

You've got to find a way out. Somehow. But how?

You can't move forward. You can't move backward.

You squeeze your eyes shut and struggle against the invisible field. But it seems to be getting stronger the harder you fight. Frustrated, you let your body go limp.

And then you notice something. The areas where your muscles are totally relaxed aren't tingling quite so much! Maybe that's the key! Maybe the force field is activated by your fear!

You flop onto the stairs. You close your eyes. You concentrate on fun, happy things. Cake with ice cream. Swimming in the ocean. Playing baseball with your friends.

You start to fall down the stairs. You did it! You freed yourself! You breathe a long sigh of relief. Then you scramble down the stairs and return to the living room.

Go to PAGE 11.

You've decided to escape. Marcie's aim is too good with that flyswatter. You swoop out of the living room as fast as you can.

Marcie's right behind you, chasing you down a narrow hallway. You come to a dead end.

Desperately, you try to duck past her. The open window you used before was in the living room. No way you'll get back to it now.

"I'm not a bat!" you squeak again, but you know it's hopeless.

"Come back here!" Marcie shouts. She swats at you again, brushing one of your wings. You stagger against a wall and almost fall to the ground.

You've got to escape from her!

You spot a staircase leading to the second floor a few feet ahead. To your left is what appears to be the kitchen.

Quick! Choose an escape route and get out of the hall!

If you fly to the kitchen, turn to PAGE 104.
If you escape up the stairs, go to PAGE 10.

"Help!" Lara shrieks. "It's got me!" She struggles as the hand begins to pull her into the ground.

"What is it?" Marcie yells, terror in her voice.

"It's a corpse!" Martin cries. "It's pulling her under!"

You throw your arms around Lara, but you're no match for the powerful creature dragging her down. A moment later, you feel something clutching your own ankle.

"No!" you scream. "No!"

You hear Marcie and Martin screaming and see that rotting hands have grabbed them, too. All four of you are being pulled deeper and deeper into the soft, rotten-smelling ground.

"Help us, Professor Krupnik!" you call. You're up to your neck in the soil. "I got them out of the house! Now save us!"

At first there is no answer. Then you hear an evil-sounding, ghostly chuckle. "Why would I want you to meet in my graveyard any more than in my mansion?" the ghost asks.

You start to protest, but your mouth is filling up with dirt. Too bad, it looks as if you learned a lesson the hard way — never trust a ghost!

THE END

"I made it!" you cry. "I'm safe!"

Then you see Nick strolling down the hallway toward you. His long reptile tail drags behind him, sending up clouds of dust.

"It's all over!" he calls triumphantly.

"What do you mean?" you cry.

"I mean — too bad," Nick sneers. "You didn't find all the items in time. You lose."

"Hold on," you protest. "I still have an hour."

"Check your watch," Nick hisses. "It's now one minute to midnight."

You gaze at your watch. "Oh, no!" you cry out. To your horror, you see that Nick is right. You were sent back an hour later than when you left!

Now you feel your teeth begin to lengthen and grow down over your lips. Enormous warts pop out all over your skin. Your body hunches and your arms sweep the ground. Sorry! The red stone wasn't much help. It returned you to your own time at the WRONG time!

THE END

You listen to the monsters talk.

"It's almost midnight," Connor says.

"Soon our friend will join us," Nick adds.

"It's good to have some new blood," Debbie agrees.

You press your ear closer and continue to listen.

"I can't believe the Horror Club has been around for five hundred years," Nick says. "We've had so many members."

"Yeah," Debbie agrees. "It's too bad we lose so many of them. I don't understand why this house turns most of our new members to stone."

Nick starts to speak again. But you stop listening. Turn to stone? Can that be true? Forget the scavenger hunt, you say to yourself. Just find a way to leave!

But you can't. You can't move. Not a muscle.

You have become strangely stiff. Your feet feel as heavy as rocks.

Then you look down to see that your feet *are* rocks!

Too bad! It looks as if the only thing left for you to do is join a rock group!

THE END

"The game is called The Hunt," Marcie tells you. "I am captain of the Blue Team. Nick is captain of the Red Team."

You watch as Nick picks Debbie and a skinny boy named Connor to be on his team. Connor has short bristly hair and a very strange smell. As Connor walks by, you decide he smells as if he's been lying in a Dumpster!

For the Blue Team, Marcie chooses a beautiful girl with long blond hair and green eyes. Her name is Lara. She smiles shyly at you. Marcie also picks the guy in the muscle shirt.

"Hi, I'm Martin," the kid says, pounding you on the back. "Welcome to the Horror Club!" He laughs, then flexes his muscles. You step back. Martin's arm is bigger than your whole body!

"That's three on each team," Marcie announces. "Our new member can join either one." She turns to you. "It's up to you. Which team will you join?"

Would you rather hang out with Nick, Debbie, and Connor on the Red Team? Or get to know Lara, Marcie, and Martin on the Blue Team?

To join the Red Team, turn to PAGE 88.
To join the Blue Team, turn to PAGE 33.

You need only one bone. You take a deep breath and grab hold of the skeleton hand. The yellowed fingers feel icy cold. You grasp the pinky and twist. It comes loose with a sickening snap. You drop it in your pocket, and try not to think about it. Too much.

You glance at the list again. Now all you have to do is find the three other items — three hairs from a werewolf, a straw from a witch's broom, and a piece from a mummy's bandage. The faster, the better, you think.

You dart out of the kitchen and return to the dining room.

"*Psst. Psst.*"

You gaze around nervously.

"Over here!" Debbie whispers from a shadowy corner.

Find out what Debbie wants on PAGE 6.

You turn to the left and jog down the narrow hallway. You listen for the three monsters. But all you hear are your own sneakers slapping against the floorboards as you run.

The end of the hall is dark — pitch-black. You wish you had a flashlight. You can't even see your own feet!

You slow down and place one hand on the wall to guide you. You wonder if you should turn back. Then you feel something — something rough and bristly.

Your fingers tighten around it. You squint in the blackness.

It's a rope. No, you realize suddenly, it's a rope *ladder*!

The ladder runs up the wall. You decide to climb it. You've got nothing to lose, you figure. And there might be a way out at the top!

You grab on tightly to the rope and begin to climb. The rope rubs roughly against your hands, making them burn, but you ignore the pain and keep climbing.

The ladder sways from side to side with each step. Your stomach lurches, but you continue on. You concentrate on not looking down.

Then you hit the final rung.

You carefully reach a hand up to the ceiling and feel a sliding door!

Open the door on PAGE 131.

You approach the heavy stone door of the crypt. Instead of a doorknob, it has a thick iron ring. Chiseled into the stone above the ring are these words:

WHO TURNS THE STONE WILL GROW BAT BONES

What could that possibly mean? you wonder. A sudden movement draws your attention. Near the top of the crypt you see a small hole — about your size. While you watch, a tiny black bat flies out of the hole and flutters off into the night.

Outrageous, you think. Maybe you can catch a bat inside the crypt. That would win the contest for sure.

But how will you get inside? The door is covered with cobwebs. Obviously, it hasn't been opened in a long time. Maybe you could climb to the top of the crypt and crawl in through the hole the bat came out of.

Or maybe you should just try to pull the big stone door open. It might work.

Which will you try?

If you crawl in through the hole, turn to PAGE 32.

If you try to open the stone door, go to PAGE 9.

You've decided to find the cemetery on your own. You're a little concerned about how the couple might react to a talking bat.

You begin to fly up, as high as you can go. Soon your whole neighborhood lies below you, as tiny as the town in a model train set. You scan the houses and streets. You have to peer hard — your bat vision isn't very good. But then you see it — the cemetery across the street from Bat Wing Hall.

You swoop toward the cemetery, but a stiff wind blows you in the other direction. You struggle to get back on course, but you're still not very good at flying.

You fight the gusty wind and finally reach the cemetery. You aim at a tree and land clumsily on the tip of a branch. You notice that the sky is beginning to grow light — you've been out all night!

You yawn, then glance around the cemetery. You spot the Krupnik Crypt behind some trees. You fly toward the crypt and notice that the door is still wide open. You swoop inside just as the sun begins to rise.

CLANG! The stone door slams shut behind you. You're trapped!

Go on to PAGE 55.

You stare at Nick, Debbie, and Connor's gruesome faces. There's no question they're monsters. Real monsters.

"Let me out of here!" you cry.

Nick still blocks the door. You spot a window in the living room. You take a deep breath and race for it.

You're fast. You always win the fifty-yard dash at school. But against these monsters, you're not fast enough.

Debbie easily beats you to the window. The tarantulas scurry through her spiderweb hair, as she cackles, "There's no way out!"

"Please, let me go home," you plead. "I won't tell anyone your secret. Just let me go."

"No way!" Nick cries, as he enters the living room with Connor. "There's no escape from the Horror Club."

"Well," Debbie says, "that's not exactly true. There is *one* way out."

You gaze around the room, searching frantically for an exit. The three monsters circle you. You don't see any way past them. "Where is it?" you ask. "How do I get out?"

Nick glares at Debbie.

"Your only hope," Debbie says, ignoring Nick, "is to play the game."

Go to PAGE 48.

You try to duck under the tidal wave of mud. But the force is too strong. You are sucked deeper and deeper into the mud.

But Nick jumps over the wave. And he makes it!

"You lost!" Nick cries in triumph.

"Wait — " you cry. "Let me — "

"Forget it!" Connor roars. "We made a deal! Now just hold still, and it will be over in a minute."

You drop your head into your hands. In a few minutes, you'll be a monster, too.

You try to look on the bright side — you'll still be able to play video games. In fact, you're ready to ask Nick for a rematch.

THE END

"Let's check out the science store," you tell your friends. Maybe there will be something there that will help you with your problem.

"Cool!" Lara exclaims. She leads the way to the upper level. A big banner hangs in front of a store declaring UNCLE ED'S SCIENCE EMPORIUM. This looks promising, you think. You push through the door, and the others follow you.

"Look at this great gear!" Martin says. "There's all kinds of kits and experiments."

"Cool!" Marcie points to an exhibit where you can examine your own fingerprints under a magnifying glass.

"What are *those*?" Lara asks. You follow her to an exhibit of tropical insects. The insects are inside a glass case. You gaze at them in fascination. They're all colors of the rainbow, and some of the beetles are as big as mice!

"Yuck!" Lara says.

You don't pay any attention. Staring at the insects has reminded you how hungry you are. Instead of flying around and eating a couple of dozen moths, you could eat just one of these beetles for a whole meal!

No, you tell yourself. *No, no, no!* But as you continue to gaze at the beetles, your mouth begins to water. Suddenly, the bat in you takes over.

Hurry to PAGE 41.

You've got to go back to the Krupnik Crypt — right now!

Luckily, your mom works on Saturday. "Are you sure you'll be all right?" she asks, poking her head into the dark bedroom before she leaves.

"I'm fine," you tell her. "Just tired." The second you hear the front door slam, you pull on a turtleneck, a heavy coat, gloves, dark glasses, and a hat. That should protect you from the sun.

Only it doesn't. You manage to get as far as the end of the driveway before your skin starts to blister.

You'll have to wait until dark.

That evening you tell your parents you're going to a movie with a friend. From the window in your room, you watch the sun sink below the horizon. As soon as it sets, you turn to leave for the mansion.

But the floor has suddenly become very far away. You watch in horror as black hairs sprout all over your arms. Your fingers stiffen, and black webs spread between them. Your mouth tingles as fangs burst through your gums. You hang your furry head as you realize the sad truth:

You're a bat — again.

Flutter to PAGE 92.

Four kids sit in a circle on the living room floor. A big yellow candle flickers in the center.

They all turn and stare at you.

No one seems happy to see you.

You stand awkwardly as Nick introduces you and says, "This is our newest member."

"What are you talking about?" cries a girl with short, curly red hair. She glares at you.

"I've brought a new member to the Horror Club," Nick repeats.

"Not today!" exclaims a large boy with bulging arm muscles.

"Why not?" Debbie asks, squirming next to you.

"Didn't anyone tell you?" asks another girl. "Tonight's the special night. You've got to get that kid out of here. We're not telling stories tonight. The plan has changed!"

Discover what's happening tonight on PAGE 128.

"What was that noise?" Lara cries, glancing up. And then she sees you. "A bat!" she shrieks. "Gross, a bat!" She jumps off her bed and tears out of the room.

A moment later she returns with a big can of bug spray.

"Get out of here!" she shrieks. She turns the nozzle at you and presses her finger down on the spray button.

You don't know if bug spray can hurt bats, and you don't want to find out. You swoop out the window before the spray can reach you.

"Don't come back!" Lara screams, slamming the window shut.

You're so upset, you can barely flap your wings as you fly home. How are you ever going to get anyone to help you? Will you have to remain a bat for the rest of your life?

You slip into your room, wondering what to do. You flutter over to your bed. There's a note on your pillow from your mom: *Lara called. Meet her at the fountain in the mall at 3:00 tomorrow.*

You immediately feel better. Lara invited you to the mall with Marcie and Martin! You've definitely been accepted by these new kids. Maybe they'll be able to help you.

All you have to do is find a way to get to the mall without being fried by the sun.

Will you be able to do it? Swoop over to PAGE 133.

"What do you mean?" you demand. "All I want to do is return to the crypt!"

"There's only one way back there," the blue head says.

"And it's extremely dangerous," the red head adds. The blue head nods in agreement.

"We can tell you how to go safely — on one condition," the blue head says. "Come with us on a tour of the library. No one has visited us since our librarian was eaten by the Swamp Thing."

You don't seem to have a choice. You follow the monsters into the library.

At first, it looks like an ordinary library, filled with bookshelves. But then you glance at the books. They're all about monsters! You see the titles *Frankenstein*, *Godzilla*, and *Dracula*. You notice a monster cookbook, a monster travel book, and monster encyclopedias.

"The best books are in the next room," the red head sneers. "Our favorite stories are all there."

But you've stopped listening. In a corner of the room, you've spotted a door labeled TO THE CRYPT. Could it be the way out?

If you make a run for the crypt, hurry to PAGE 35.

If you decide to stay and wait for the monster to help, go to PAGE 134.

You run for the dining room.

But Nick clamps a clawed, green hand on your wrist. "Afraid of a little blood? What a wimp!"

You try to struggle free, but Nick holds on tight.

"You've failed the test!" Connor announces. He points to the watch on his thick hairy wrist. "It's already one minute to midnight!"

"What?" you cry. You try to glance at your own watch, but Nick is gripping your arm too hard. "I've only started searching," you protest. "I've still got plenty of time!"

"But we're running on *monster* time!" Nick taunts with an evil grin. "And by our clock — your time has run out!"

"No!" you scream. "No!"

With all your strength you pull your arm free from Nick.

You glance at your watch.

Magically, it too reads one minute to midnight!

Then you glance at your wrist again. And scream.

Thick brown hair is growing on your arm! And your legs . . . and all over you!

And now claws are sprouting where your fingernails once were.

Too bad! From the look of it, you're on monster time now, too.

Forever!

THE END

You read the list again. Then you start to laugh. These guys really take this Horror Club stuff seriously, you think. Still laughing, you point to the list and say, "Great joke. Very funny."

"Why are you laughing?" Connor demands.

"This list — it's a riot," you reply. You wonder why no one else has even cracked a smile.

"It's not a joke," Nick insists. "That's the list for our scavenger hunt."

"Give me a break," you say. "You expect me to believe that? Where would I find those things?"

"In this house," Debbie replies matter-of-factly.

"Yeah, right," you scoff. "I'm supposed to believe that there really are werewolves, and witches, and mummies?"

"It's true," Connor says.

"Do you want me to prove it?" Nick asks with an evil grin. A very evil grin.

What is Nick up to? Turn to PAGE 47.

80

You dash toward the mummy case. You quickly jump in and slam the lid shut. You stand stiffly in the darkness, scarcely daring to breathe. Waiting.

You can hear the king's guards coming closer. Did they see you hide?

No! Their footsteps thunder past you, and you exhale with relief.

You wait several minutes, wondering if it is okay to climb out. You decide to wait a little bit more, when the lid suddenly springs open.

You poke your head out in terror.

But no one's there — and the blue sky and flowers are gone! You're in a dimly lit hallway.

You step out and almost knock into a mummy. A *sleeping* mummy!

"Oh, no!" you cry out. "I'm back in Bat Wing Hall."

You glance at your watch. Only half an hour left before you turn into a monster! You have to complete the scavenger hunt! You've got to get moving!

You need to grab a piece of the sleeping mummy's bandage. There's no time to waste!

Turn to PAGE 39.

"I'll help you," you tell Professor Krupnik.

"Good," the ghost growls. "Now get these kids out of Bat Wing Hall. And make sure they never come back."

It's weird that a ghost would need your help. But you do as Professor Krupnik asks. When you get to the mansion, you peer in through a window and see Marcie, Martin, and Lara sitting on the floor and talking.

How can you make them leave?

You know that it will be hard to scare them away. After all, they're members of the Horror Club. But maybe it would be different if they knew that the house really *is* haunted.

Or — maybe it would be better to come up with a better place for the Horror Club to meet.

Which will it be?

To convince them the house is haunted, turn to PAGE 15.

Or to get them to move to a new place, go to PAGE 130.

You watch, horrified, as the red sun sinks into the distance. At the same moment, you feel hairs sprouting all over your body. Your shoulders start to ache as your arms turn into bat wings. A moment later, you're hovering over the heads of your friends.

Lara lets out a scream. Marcie's jaw has dropped open so wide you can see her fillings. Martin looks impressed.

"Did you see what happened?" Marcie exclaims. "The story was true!"

"I wouldn't believe it if I hadn't seen it!" Martin says.

"Did you say you need our help?" Lara asks you. She seems frightened, but also concerned.

"I need you to help me close the Krupnik Crypt," you squeak. But they can't understand your bat language.

How can you get them to help you now? You start to fly across the street, toward the cemetery. Your friends only watch you, puzzled.

"Maybe it's hungry," Lara suggests. "Should we catch some insects for it?"

Frustrated, you fly back to your waiting friends. Again, you fly toward the cemetery, again you return.

"I know what it's doing!" Martin says suddenly.

Can Martin help you? Turn to PAGE 46.

Your heart thuds as you approach the closet door. The pool of blood grows larger on the floor. Slowly, you pull the door open.

And gasp.

There's no dead body in the closet. No dead anything. Only a broken jar. A jar of raspberry jam, dripping onto the floor.

You sigh with relief and explore the closet further. The shelves are crammed with rusty cans of vegetables and moldy sacks of flour. You quickly search all the shelves, but find nothing.

Then you spot it. A plastic shoe box on the bottom shelf.

You reach down and open it. You can't believe your eyes!

Nestled in the center of the box, on a dark piece of cloth, is the skeleton of a human hand!

"Oh, gross," you moan. You try not to wonder whose hand it was and how it got in this box.

"You found our skeleton in the closet!" Debbie sings out.

You nod. You're glad you found something on the list, but you don't want to touch the hand. You start to carry the box away from the closet. But Nick stops you.

"The list says *one* bone from a human hand, not the whole hand," he reminds you. His reptile tongue darts in and out of his mouth.

You stare down at the hand. One bone!

Rattle over to PAGE 67.

"I choose the glowing red stone," you tell the wizard.

Silently the wizard hands it to you.

The red stone is strangely warm in your hand, and it seems to be vibrating. You can feel its slow throbbing.

As you stare at the stone, it glows brighter and brighter. The heat from the stone seeps through your hand, spreading warmth to your arm. Then to your whole body.

You begin to sweat. Your temperature rises.

The priests begin chanting.

You grow hotter. Hotter. Hotter!

The chanting voices fade in and out.

I'm burning up! you think frantically.

A yellow light suddenly flashes before your eyes. The light is so incredibly bright you have to shut your eyes.

When you open them, you are in a dark hallway. And your body feels okay. Not too hot. Not too cold.

You gaze around in amazement.

You are back in Bat Wing Hall! You're safe!

Go to PAGE 64.

Nick's just trying to scare you, you think. He's testing you, to see if you're brave enough for the Horror Club.

You shrug and rush forward. You dash across the porch and squeeze through a narrow space in the boards covering the front door. You land on your knees with a thud.

As soon as you hit the floor, a piercing alarm sounds through the house. What's going on? you wonder.

You gaze around quickly. Nick and Debbie are nowhere to be found. The dark house seems empty. You hold your ears, trying to block out the horrible noise. And then, through a dusty window, you see lights. Red, whirling lights.

The police!

You have set off a burglar alarm. Now you're in big trouble! How will you ever explain this to the police — or to your mom and dad?

Too bad! It looks as if your adventure is over even before it began!

THE END

"I'm going to trust you," you tell Debbie. "Please help me get out of here!"

"A wise choice!" Debbie sneers. She glances over her shoulder, then beckons you to follow her. "Be quiet," she warns. "There's no telling what Nick and Connor will do if they find out!"

You creep down a long dark hall behind Debbie. The tarantulas squirm wildly through her hair. You are glad Debbie, with her gross purple face, is really a friend.

Then you reach the end of the hall.

And there stand Nick and Connor. Saliva drips from their mouths as they smack their lips.

Then seven-foot-tall Connor lumbers toward you. His enormous arms reach for you.

You glance back at Debbie for help.

She's your friend — right?

Hurry to PAGE 38.

You follow the left-hand path along the river. The whole time you wonder: Where am I? How will I ever get home?

You feel eyes on you — creatures' eyes. Staring at you. You whirl around, searching, but you see no one.

Then you hear a sound you can't ignore. Footsteps. Heavy, heavy footsteps. The footsteps of something very big. And very, very close. *THUMP . . . THUMP . . . THUMP . . .*

You freeze. The footsteps stop. You glance behind you, but all you can see is the swirling mist.

Maybe it was nothing. You start up again, but so do the steps! *THUMP . . . THUMP . . . THUMP!* They're getting closer. You don't dare look back.

You try to run, but your feet sink into the marshy ground. The thing is almost right behind you!

And then, just ahead, you spot a cave. You can hide in there. You race to the cave. A sign beside it says MONSTER LIBRARY. You have no idea what a Monster Library is, but you don't care. Anything would be better than this swamp with a *thing* following you. You duck inside.

Oh, no! The thing behind you runs in, too.

Race to PAGE 119.

"I choose the Red Team," you announce.

"Fine," Marcie says. "The Red Team will stay in the house for the games. The Blue Team will go outside. See you later!"

Marcie, Lara, and Martin leave the house.

You turn to your new teammates with a smile. You're looking forward to the games.

"I'm glad you're on our team," Nick says. "We're having a scavenger hunt. Everything has to be found inside the house."

"Cool," you reply. "I love scavenger hunts. Where's the list?"

"Here it is," Debbie says, handing you a piece of white paper.

You read the list of items out loud:

"HORROR CLUB SCAVENGER HUNT
— one human bone
— three hairs from a werewolf
— a straw from a witch's broom
— a piece from a mummy's bandage."

Go to PAGE 79.

There's no way you're hanging around with some Egyptian king!

"Thanks for the invitation," you say politely, "but I'd like to leave."

The king shows you to the door, and you step outside, into a beautiful garden filled with flowers. Red, purple, orange — flowers of every kind, in every hue. The sky shines a brilliant blue, and you fill your lungs with the sweet-smelling air. You want to jump for joy.

You spot something familiar in the distance, something leaning against a tree. A mummy case! It looks like the same mummy case you found in Bat Wing Hall.

"Get him! There he is!" someone shouts from behind you.

You reel around — it's the king. Uh-oh, you mumble to yourself. Looks as if the king changed his mind.

His men come charging toward you. You gaze frantically around the garden. At the far edge is a thicket of tall reeds. You could hide there.

Quick! Do something!

To hide in the mummy case, go to PAGE 80.
To run for the reeds, race to PAGE 99.

Nick begins his story. "There once were three kids. They looked like kids you'd meet every day at school or in the playground. But these kids were different. They were under an evil spell — a spell that turned them into monsters. And there was only one way to release them from it."

"What's that?" Connor asks, leaning forward.

"They had to find another kid who would pass a horrible, deadly test. No kid had ever completed the test and lived to tell about it," Nick continues in a low voice. "The test was a scavenger hunt, and the kid would have to find four creepy — impossible — things. Only then would the monsters change back to kids."

"What happened?" Debbie asks breathlessly.

You stand up and head for the front door. You're going home. You have a funny feeling you know exactly how this story is going to

END

Great choice!

Now you're stuck at home with nothing to do. Sure, you can clean out your closet. Or play stupid board games with your little brother. But that doesn't change things.

You still have no friends. You're still bored.

But wait — you have one last chance!

You hurry to the big yellow phone book. You look up Nick's phone number. You grab the phone and dial. It rings. And rings.

And then you hear Nick's voice. "Hello?"

Finish your conversation on PAGE 17.

You don't want to spend the rest of your life as a bat. You've got to get to the crypt. You decide to fly. Luckily, the window is slightly open. You duck through it and glide out into the cool evening air.

You realize you need to practice using your wings. First you try flapping, then you soar up and down. It's kind of fun, dipping and swooping over the backyard.

You also like your cool sonar system. Through your super bat's ears, you're able to hear thousands of times better than you could as a human. Insects sound as loud as cars did when you were a kid.

Something makes a flapping sound to your right. Without even looking, your sonar tells you it's a gnat. A thundering buzz, like the sound of a chain saw, comes from a june bug. You can not only tell *what* the insects are, you can tell *where* they are.

Your sonar informs you that a large moth is fluttering in the trees just ahead. The thought of the moth makes your mouth water. You realize you're very, very hungry.

A *moth*? You're going to eat a moth?

To find out what a moth tastes like, turn to PAGE 137.

"Lara!" You call. "Martin! Marcie!"

The only answer is the wind rustling through the trees. Your eyes search the cemetery, but your gaze falls only on crumbling headstones. You glance across the street at the mansion, but it's completely dark. Has everyone gone home?

Another bat flies by and you decide not to wait around. You race out of the cemetery and head for home.

Later that night, you don't feel very well. Your shoulders ache and your fingers feel stiff.

Maybe you're getting sick. You hope not. You don't want to miss soccer practice. You climb into bed and drift into a troubled sleep. When you awaken a few hours later, it's still dark, and you feel even worse.

Maybe a drink of water would make you feel better. As you get up, you notice that your hands seem to be very stiff. You glance down and see something dark between all your fingers.

It must be the shadows in the room, you think. Your feet don't seem to be working very well, but somehow you make your way to the bathroom. You reach up to flip on the light. But the light switch isn't where it's supposed to be.

Instead, it's three feet above you! And the bathroom mirror is even higher.

What's going on? Hurry! Turn to PAGE 124.

You hurry down the hall after the mummy. There's not much time. You still need three more items for the scavenger hunt. There doesn't seem to be any other way to get out of Bat Wing Hall.

As you continue, the putrid smell grows stronger.

Then, at the end of the hall, you see a beautiful, gold mummy case. And leaning against the wall beside it is the mummy!

The mummy's head rests on the case. Strange snorting noises come from under its bandages. With a start, you realize that the noises are snores. The mummy is asleep!

You know that a piece of a mummy's bandage is on the list. But what's the best way to get one?

You spot some torn pieces of bandage inside the mummy case. Should you take a piece from there?

Or should you try to pull a strip off of the sleeping mummy?

Either way, you'd better hurry. It's less than an hour until midnight!

To take a piece of bandage from the case, turn to PAGE 117.

To tear a strip off the mummy, sneak over to PAGE 39.

"Okay," you tell the witch. "I'll try to help you."

"You won't regret it," she promises. "Hurry around to the back of the box."

You do as she says. On the back of the clear box are two hand prints. "Place your hands on the prints," the witch instructs. Once again, you follow her request.

"Now repeat after me: *Arikarem. Amikaroo.*"

You chant the magic words.

"Now clap your hands," she says. You clap.

Nothing happens. You clap again. Still nothing.

"What's going on?" you demand impatiently.

"I must have given you the wrong spell," she admits. "I'm a little rusty with my magic after all these years. Now *what* were those words?"

"Hurry!" you cry. It's ten minutes until midnight! You try to pull your hands away from the box. But they are stuck — as if they were glued! "Hurry," you urge her again.

"I've got it!" she announces. "Say the words: *Spmubesoog. Spmubesoog.*"

You notice the witch has her fingers crossed — not a good sign! You repeat the magic words.

Go to PAGE 18.

A huge, dark shadow looms at the end of the street. It's the mansion.

You stop walking and gaze up at it. Nick shines his flashlight at the old house on the hill.

Bat Wing Hall is a two-story, old-fashioned house. All the windows that aren't boarded up are broken. Loose shingles flap from the roof. Paint peels from the weathered sides of the house. It looks as if no one has lived here for hundreds of years.

You climb up to the sagging porch with Nick and Debbie. Tall, overgrown trees and bushes cast eerie shadows across the deserted lawn.

"Isn't this place awesome?" Debbie whispers to you.

"Really cool," you agree.

"This house has been empty for two years," Nick tells you. "Ever since crazy old Professor Krupnik died."

"No one will buy it because it's haunted," Debbie explains. You notice she's chewing nervously at the ends of her long hair. Yuck!

"The front door was boarded up until we figured out how to pry it open," Debbie says. She points to the large wooden door. "Let's go."

You take a step forward.

"Stop!" Nick shouts. "Get down! Now!"

If you do as Nick says, hurry to PAGE 19.

If you ignore him and head for the door, go to PAGE 85.

It's a huge black rat — and it scurries across your sneaker! You jump back and scream.

You can hear the rat's sharp claws scratch across the floorboards as it disappears into the living room. You wonder what other gross creatures are crawling around this old house.

You decide to head into the kitchen. *Clomp. Clomp. Clomp.* You can hear Nick, Debbie, and Connor following you.

"If you're afraid of a little rat," Nick hisses in your ear, "then you're going to be in big trouble later. Big trouble."

You try to ignore Nick, even though your knees shake at his warning. You spot a kerosene lamp on the kitchen table. You pick it up so you can see into the dark corners of the kitchen better.

The kitchen is filled with cupboards, closets, and shelves. Anything could be hidden here!

You pull open drawer after drawer. Clouds of dust make your eyes itch.

Then in the next drawer you open, you see them.

Bandages! But are these mummy's bandages?

You hope they are, shoving several in your pocket. One item off the list, you think.

Then a hideous scream cuts through the air.

Run to PAGE 12.

You fly toward the ring and perch on it. You take a moment to look each of your friends directly in the eyes.

"You have to turn the ring!" you instruct. "You have to close the door to the crypt!"

"What's it squeaking about?" Martin asks.

"I don't know," Lara replies. "But it seems to have something to do with the ring on the door."

Marcie has been peering intently at the door. "I think this door used to be closed," she says. "Maybe that's what it's telling us. Maybe it wants us to shut the door."

"Yes, yes, yes!" you squeak. You're so happy you could kiss her, but you figure it would gross her out.

Marcie begins to push on the door. It barely budges.

"Let me help!" says Martin. He pushes, too, and then Lara joins in, but the door hardly moves.

"It's too heavy!" Marcie complains. "We can't shut it."

Oh, no! What are you going to do?

Go to PAGE 25.

You run as fast as you can into the thicket of tall reeds. Then you duck down and gaze through the tall stalks.

The guards have stopped. They appear to be arguing. One of them points to the thicket. Oh, no! But the others shake their heads violently. They turn around and head back for the palace.

What happened? you wonder. Why won't they go into the thicket?

You shrug and decide not to worry about it. You have more important things to think about — like how to get home!

Suddenly, you hear a rustling noise. In fact, you think, it sounds more like a rattle. You glance down and let out a wail of terror!

A huge black snake is coiled at your feet!

The snake's leathery body is thicker than your two legs put together!

The snake lifts its head and hisses. Then it opens its mouth. Wider. Wider. Wider. Its long tongue uncurls and darts out at you. Oh, no! The snake is going to swallow you whole!

Go to PAGE 110.

"Haunted? For real?" you ask.

"For real," Nick replies seriously. "That's why we picked it. Some of the scariest stories I've ever heard happened in Bat Wing Hall."

"Like what?"

"Like the story of the kids on Halloween night," Nick says. "They were all dressed up. Trick-or-treating. They rang Krupnik's doorbell. A figure dressed all in black answered, and the kids were invited inside . . . only they *never* came out!"

"What happened?" you ask breathlessly.

"Nobody knows," Nick replies. "But late at night you can still hear the kids' screams. Horrible screams. And when the moon is full — some people say they've seen little creatures in monster costumes roaming about inside the house! Trapped. Forever!"

"Wow! Great story!" you say.

"It's *not* a story," Nick tells you. "Being a member of the Horror Club can be dangerous. *Very* dangerous." He pauses, then adds, "Today is Friday. We meet tonight. Do you want to come?"

What do you think?

Risk it and go to the Horror Club tonight, turn to PAGE 17.

Say thanks anyway and go to PAGE 91.

You decide to try to act like a wolf.

Very carefully, you drop the broom. Then you get down on your hands and knees. The werewolf backs off, confused.

So far, so good, you think. You tilt your head back and howl. A long mournful howl.

The werewolf howls back!

You start to crawl toward the beast, sniffing the ground like an animal. You glance up. The werewolf is staring at you intently. Will he attack? you wonder.

You continue with your wolf act. You crawl until you are just inches away from him. You raise your head again when — he pounces!

The beast knocks you to the ground. You stare up in terror. His vicious fangs are less than an inch from your face! His mouth opens —

And then he starts to lick your nose!

He thinks you are another werewolf. He likes you — a lot! He licks your cheeks, your nose, your neck, your fur. Fur?

You hear the last gong of a chiming clock in the distance. And Nick, Debbie, and Connor's uproarious laughter. With a sinking heart, you realize it is midnight. The game is over.

You acted your part well. Too well. Now you're a werewolf forever! Well, at least you made a friend!

THE END

102

You remember the Krupnik Crypt. And that the only *living* creature you saw was the bat that flew out of the tomb. With a gnawing fear, your mind plays over the words carved in the crypt: WHO TURNS THE STONE WILL GROW BAT BONES.

You should have realized it was a warning. But no, you had to go ahead and turn that stupid stone!

That must have been how this happened. You try frantically to remember everything about the crypt, any little detail that could help you. You picture the crypt and suddenly recall that you'd left the stone door open. Maybe if you turn the stone again — closing the door of the crypt — you'll be transformed back.

Should you return to the cemetery now? You're not sure you can even find it in the dark.

Or would it be better to go to sleep and wait until morning? Maybe when you wake up, you'll be back to normal.

If you return to the cemetery now, hurry to PAGE 27.

If you wait until morning, turn to PAGE 53.

It's amazing! Marcie, Lara, and Martin are acting as if they see ghosts every day. So much for scaring them out of the mansion! You need a new plan.

Lara eyes Professor Krupnik. "What's it like to be a ghost?" she asks. The ghost seems startled by the question.

"It's . . . it's . . ." he stammers.

Now Marcie and Martin swarm around him, firing questions at him. "Can you appear in other forms?" "How long have you been a ghost?" "What do you do all day?"

To your amazement, the ghost starts to smile. He holds up his shadowy hands. "Slow down. I can answer only one question at a time."

He actually seems to be enjoying the attention! Maybe it's lonely being a ghost. You get a great idea.

"Fellow teammates," you announce. "I nominate Professor Krupnik as the newest member of the Horror Club." When you see the grin on the ghost's face, you know this was the perfect solution.

Just in time, too. After a unanimous vote, Professor Krupnik mutters some strange words and waves his arms. Whatever he did, it worked! The sun drops below the horizon — and you're still a kid! You settle down to listen to the ghost's scary stories, thrilled that this adventure has come to a happy

END

As fast as you can fly, you head for the kitchen. "Stop!" Marcie shrieks, running after you.

There's got to be a way out! Your heart and wings are beating furiously as you search the kitchen. But the door and all the windows are shut. The only other way out is the doorway you flew in — and Marcie's standing there with the flyswatter!

"I'm not really a bat!" you plead as loudly as you can. "I've been transformed!"

"You filthy beast!" Marcie screams. She heads straight for you, the flyswatter raised, ready to smash you. She manages to whack you, hard. You bang into the wall, your head spinning. One more blow like that, and it will be all over. Oh, no! Here she comes again! Your eyes dart all around the room.

Just ahead you notice a large, standing freezer. It's open just a crack. In desperation, you fly into the crack.

"I've got you now!" Marcie cries, and slams the freezer shut.

"Hey!" you call. "Let me out of here!"

But there's no answer. Marcie won't let you out, you realize, until you're frozen solid.

Too bad, but you made the wrong choice. And it looks as if you'll end this adventure as a batsicle!

THE END

"I have all the items on the list," you announce as you enter the dark living room. "I found the human bone, mummy's bandage, the witch's broom, and I even got three hairs from a were — "

"What are you talking about?" Nick interrupts.

You gasp. You can't believe your eyes.

There sit Nick, Debbie, and Connor in a circle on the living room floor. But they're not monsters! They look like normal kids!

"What happened?" you cry. "Why did you change back?"

"Change back?" Debbie asks, running a hand through her long — spider-free — hair. "Change back from what?"

"From monsters," you say. "Come on, you guys. I know what you really are. Don't play any more games."

"Hey, Nick," Connor says. "Your new friend is nuts. Monsters! Ha! That's a good one."

"But — but the scavenger hunt. And the mummy and the skeleton," you try to explain. The three kids stare at you with blank expressions as you stammer.

"Listen," Debbie tells you, standing up and leading you to their circle. "You're just in time for Nick's very spooky story."

You sit on the floor, your mind spinning.

Turn to PAGE 90.

106

They want you to search the cemetery all by yourself. You're about to say *No way, José*, but then you figure that's just what they expect you to do.

You'll show them!

"Great!" you declare. "I bet I'll find the winning object." You even kind of mean it. After all, if the game is won by finding the scariest stuff, then your teammates just handed you an easy score. What better place to look than a cemetery? You give your teammates the thumbs up, and hurry across the street.

The cemetery is really old, and most of the gravestones are chipped and crumbling. As you stumble over a lumpy grave, you feel something grab at your ankle! You yelp and jump back.

Phew! It was just a gnarled root.

The moonlight casts an eerie glow, creating strange shadows. You carefully make your way toward a small building. There's just enough light for you to read the words KRUPNIK CRYPT carved in the stone over the doorway.

Here's your chance to impress your new friends. You know you will find something scary inside a crypt. But do you have the nerve to enter?

Find out on PAGE 69.

"What?" you cry.

"I've been imprisoned in this magic box for two centuries," the witch goes on. "All this time I've waited for someone to set me free."

"Really?" you say doubtfully. This sounds a lot like those fairy tales your mom used to read to you when you were five years old.

"Please help me," the woman pleads.

You glance at your watch. And then over to the broom. "I'd like to help you," you say. "But I have to find a straw from a witch's broom really fast. Otherwise, I'll turn into a monster."

"Well, I'm a witch," the woman tells you. "And I have a broom. Help me, and I'll help you."

"If you're a witch, can't you say a spell to escape?" you ask.

"Don't you think I've already tried that?" the witch spits back. "It didn't work."

Your gaze travels from the witch to the broom and back to your watch. Only fifteen minutes until midnight. What should you do?

If you choose to help the witch, go to PAGE 95.
If you decide to leave her in the box and grab her broom, go to PAGE 44.

"Let's go to the movie," you suggest. It will give you time to think of a way to ask for help.

You line up for tickets and popcorn and then settle into your seats. "This movie is supposed to be really scary," Lara says with a shiver.

As soon as the lights start to dim, you feel a familiar ache in your shoulders. With horror, you look down at your hands. The webbing is growing in between your fingers!

"I'm going to the bathroom," you mumble, and quickly jump out of your seat. The next instant, you're a bat!

You can't stay in the aisle of the theater where someone could step on you, so you fly up to the ceiling. Down below you hear laughter.

"Look at that!" someone cries. "A real bat! It must be a part of the movie!"

"What a publicity stunt," someone shouts.

Will you *tell* your friends the truth about what happened to you now?

Or would it be better to *show* them — back at Bat Wing Hall?

If you tell them now, go to PAGE 22.

If you think it's wiser to show them, fly to PAGE 45.

You run to the mansion as fast as you can. You don't want to find out who or *what* would make a sound like that! When you've put some distance between you and the voice, you glance back. Nothing. Maybe you were just imagining things.

Just to be safe, though, you quickly pull the boards away from the door and enter Bat Wing Hall. You find a good spot to hide, behind a tattered armchair — why take chances? You curl up and wait.

Your aching muscles tell you you've been sitting there for a lot longer than an hour. Peering through the smudgy windows, you can see the sun has dropped low on the horizon.

What if your friends don't show up until after you've turned back into a bat?

Turn to PAGE 14.

The snake's sharp fangs begin to drip with deadly venom.

You start to back away.

"Don't move!" a voice behind you cries.

You freeze. And then you hear music. A strange, joyous melody.

The snake seems to hear the music, too. Its head starts to sway back and forth, back and forth. Almost as if it were dancing.

"Move away slowly now," the voice instructs you. You do as you're told and bump into a small round man playing a wooden flute.

The man stops playing, and the snake slithers away.

"It is very stupid to enter the thicket of the snake," the man says. "You must be new here."

"I don't belong here at all," you tell him. "I ended up here by accident."

"This has happened before," the man replies. "And I bet the priests want to turn you into a mummy — right?"

"Yes," you cry. "What can I do?"

"I'm afraid things look hopeless for you," he says, shaking his head. "There's only one way out."

What is it? Find out on PAGE 125.

"Upstairs," you tell the monsters. "I'll search there first."

Connor begins laughing. A low, deep laugh. "Did you hear that?" he tells the others. "Upstairs! This should be good!"

Have you made the wrong choice? you wonder. It doesn't matter. You have to do something. You cross your fingers that there may be a way to escape upstairs — a way out of this house of horrors.

You head toward the main staircase in the front hall. There's no electricity in the old mansion. Your shadow flickers in the spooky light of kerosene lanterns.

Debbie follows close behind you. You pick up your pace — just in case one of those huge tarantulas decides to jump from her hair to yours!

The stairs are covered with a thick layer of dust. Slowly you start to climb. One step. Then another. The wooden boards creak and groan under your weight. The staircase stretches upward into total darkness.

Behind you, the three monsters noisily whisper to each other. You don't know what they're saying — and you don't care. You just want to get out of here — now!

You take a deep breath. It's time.

Time to — escape!

You sprint forward.

Run to PAGE 28.

You decide your best bet is to fly into the crypt. You hope your friends will get the idea to shut the door. First, you swoop around the door to the crypt.

"What's it doing?" Lara asks her friends.

"I think it's trying to tell us the door is important," Marcie says.

"Yes!" you squeak. This might actually work! You fly into the crypt. Then you fly out again.

Martin cries, "I get it! We're supposed to close the door!"

You squeak happily and nod. You fly out of the crypt and watch while Martin grasps the ring then pushes the door.

Clang! The door slams shut. But nothing happens. Then you feel a tingling sensation in your wings. A moment later, you're standing on the ground. You're a kid again!

"Hooray!" you cry. "It worked!"

"Cool!" Marcie says. "But where did Martin go?"

You glance all around, but there's no sign of your friend.

"Oh, no!" Lara suddenly cries. "Look!"

Your eyes follow where she's pointing. You see a large bat above your heads. It's fluttering very strangely, as if it doesn't really know how to fly. Uh-oh.

Get the bad news on PAGE 56.

It's probably not a good idea to ignore a command like that. Your heart thudding in your chest, you stop and turn in the direction of the voice.

At first you're surprised that the figure before you is just an old man with a long white beard. You're a little embarrassed that you were so afraid. But then you notice that the old guy's shape keeps shifting, as if he were made out of gray mist. And your jaw drops when you realize you can see right through him.

"I am the spirit of Professor Krupnik!" the old man bellows. He glares at you. "You've been disturbing my peace for the last two years! Now I will get my revenge!"

You can't believe it! You're face-to-face with a ghost — and it's mad at you!

"I haven't done anything!" you quake. "I moved to town only last week!"

"Do you deny that you're a member of the Horror Club?!" the professor thunders.

"Well, but . . . but . . ." you stammer. "But I just joined — "

"Silence!" the ghost shouts. "I've heard enough!" It reaches out for you. You feel an icy chill throughout your body.

Is this the end?

Quick! Turn to PAGE 57.

You turn and sprint for the front door.

But the entrance is blocked by Connor. He grabs your shoulder. And you nervously stare up at him — way up.

Connor has turned into a seven-foot-tall giant with one red eye in the middle of his forehead. And the stench coming off his body is unbearable!

"Where are you going?" he growls.

"I, uh, I need to go home," you mumble. You duck under Connor's massive arm and lunge for the doorknob.

And miss.

The monster that used to be Nick beat you to it. Nick locks the door and says, "Not so fast! It's time for the scavenger hunt."

Scavenger hunt? There's no way you're sticking around to play a game with monsters!

Unless this is all a joke. Hey, that's it, you think. It's all a joke. They must be wearing monster costumes.

No! you think again. They can't be wearing costumes. They're way too real-looking.

Quick — you have to make up your mind!
If you're sure it's all a joke, turn to PAGE 13.
If you believe the monsters are real, go to PAGE 71.

You decide not to risk breaking off a straw.

You stand in front of the tiny elevator with the broom. You scratch your head. The broom is definitely too tall. And the elevator opening is too short. How will you possibly make this broom fit? you wonder.

Time is ticking away. You have only one choice. You turn the broom diagonally and try to wedge it through the elevator door. It works!

You quickly jump into the elevator yourself — and the floor drops out from beneath your feet! The broom tumbles down the elevator shaft.

You grab for the railing on the elevator wall. There's nothing between you and the basement but air! You hang on, gripping so tightly your knuckles turn white.

What will you do now? There's no way you can crawl back out. And if you let go, you'll plunge to your death.

"Help!" you cry out. "Help!" But you know no one will help you.

Your fingers start to slip. You try to grip the railing more tightly. But one finger falls away. Then another . . .

Quick! Turn to PAGE 49.

116

You spin around to see who's clutching your shoulder and can't believe your eyes!

It's a one-handed skeleton!

Your heart begins to pound and your bones begin to rattle — louder than a skeleton's bones! You're terrified, but you're angry too. You won that game, fair and square. You deserve to leave.

You kick the skeleton in the shin bone — hard! His hand drops from your shoulder, as he grabs his leg and shrieks in pain.

You jerk the door open and race outside. You sprint down the street. Up your driveway. Into your nice safe house.

You made it out of Bat Wing Hall!

You practically crawl into your living room. Your little brother is sitting on the floor, a video-game control in his hand. He's playing *Mud Monsters*!

"Play with me," he begs.

"Sure!" you say. Little brother — watch out!

Up, down, jump! Left, right — *SPLAT!*

The Mud Monster destroys you with a super mud ball.

Oh, well. You win some. You lose some!

THE END

You decide to take a piece of bandage from the mummy case. You tiptoe toward the case. You hold your breath as you pass the sleeping mummy. You know it would be disastrous to wake him.

You spot a torn piece of yellowed bandage caught in a crack in the bottom of the case. You bend over. Your fingers wrap around the fabric. And a bony hand smashes through the bottom of the case and grabs your wrist!

"Ahhh!" you scream as you try to wrench free. But the hand has an iron grip. It's pulling you. Pulling you into the mummy case. You kick wildly. You scream and scream. But it's no use. You're in the mummy case now. And then the lid slams shut!

Your chest tightens. You begin to sweat. The little bit of air in the case is hot and stale. I'm going to suffocate, you think.

You bang frantically on the lid of the case.

"Help!" you cry. "Help!" But you know there's no way the three monsters are going to save you.

You pound on the lid again. And, to your surprise, it opens!

Turn to PAGE 37.

You fly through the neighborhood, checking out mailboxes. At last you find a box with Lara's last name on it. You glide up to the house, and you see Lara sitting on her bed with the phone beside her. The window's open, but you don't want to fly in and freak her out.

You land quietly on the windowsill when she's not looking. You sneak in and perch on a picture frame above Lara's bed and watch.

She punches a number into the phone. "Hello, Marcie?" she says. "It's Lara. Uh-huh. Right. I've got a cool idea. Can you meet me at the mall tomorrow? Great. Three o'clock at the fountain, okay? 'Bye."

She hangs up and punches in another number. This time she talks to Martin. She tells him to meet her at the mall, too. Now she punches in another, shorter number.

"Hello, Information?" she says. "I'd like the number of someone who just moved to town." She tells the operator your name, and writes down the number.

This is great! Lara is going to call you! You like her best of all the kids you've met. Finally, you're making friends in this town.

"I'm right here!" you squeak from the picture frame.

Turn to PAGE 76.

A bony hand grabs your shoulder.

You turn to face the thing that's got you and let out a scream.

An eight-foot-tall monster is clutching your shoulder. A monster with two hideous heads. One head is blue, with a yellow eye in the middle of its forehead. The other head is red and has huge, six-inch fangs. They are both staring at you.

You pull away from the horrible creature. Doesn't it know staring is rude?

"Where do you think you're going?" the blue head rumbles.

"The — the Monster Library," you gasp.

"You must have a card to enter," the red head snaps.

"Sorry, I didn't know," you tell it. "Besides, I'm just trying to get back home."

"Where is that?" the red head demands.

"I came here from the Krupnik Crypt," you reply.

"The Krupnik Crypt!" the blue head cries. "Then you're in worse trouble than you think!"

What could be worse than being trapped by a two-headed monster?

Find out on PAGE 77.

The king points to the instruments. "First we need to remove your brain."

"My brain?" you screech.

"Yes," the king says calmly. "The skinny hook is pushed up your nose until it reaches your brain. Then we wiggle the hook back and forth. Back and forth. To make your brain mushy."

You break out in a cold sweat. Your heart hammers away in your chest as the king continues to explain.

"Then we take the long spoon, slide it up your nose, and scoop your brain out — a little bit at a time."

Your stomach feels like it's about to heave. No, this can't be happening to me! you think.

You flail about wildly, trying to escape.

"Now don't make a fuss," the king says. "It is a great honor." Then the king nods to the priests, and they begin to unroll the bandages.

Too bad! It looks as if this time you've gotten a little too wrapped up in your adventure!

THE END

Nick suddenly whirls around and spots you! "What are you looking at?" he snarls. His long forked tongue darts out at you.

You ignore him. "Hey, Connor," you call to the giant monster. "You'd get more points if you squash the grapes *before* you get the apples."

"Who asked you?" Connor booms. But he clicks the control in hand and tries your suggestion. "It worked!" he cries in surprise. Then he grumbles, "Must have been a lucky guess."

"Not at all," you tell him. "You just stink at this game."

"What?" Connor roars. He bolts out of his chair. His head brushes the ceiling. "Why, you puny little — "

"You're so lousy at the game anyone could beat you," you go on. "Even me!"

Connor's face turns red. His giant arms reach for you.

You dodge them. "Are you afraid to play me?" you continue, even though your knees are shaking.

As you had hoped, Connor grows angrier. And angrier.

"I'm not afraid of anything!" he roars.

"Then let's have a contest," you offer. "Whoever gets the most points wins. If I win, you have to let me go. If you win, you can turn me into a monster right now. Okay?"

What will Connor say? Find out on PAGE 7.

You have a plan. You'll command the werewolf as if he were a dog. You know from training your own dog, Spots, that it is important to be firm — show the dog that you're the boss.

You hold the broom out in front of you and step forward boldly. You stare the werewolf in the eye.

"SIT!" you instruct in your most commanding voice.

The werewolf snarls. But then he sits.

"Good boy!" You try not to get too excited. "Now STAY!"

The werewolf eyes you but doesn't move a muscle.

"Good!" you praise. Now the hard part. Will you be able to pluck hairs from the beast without him biting your head off?

BONG . . . BONG . . . your heart jumps as you recognize the sound of the clock chiming. Chiming midnight!

BONG . . . BONG . . . you've got to move fast!

You step closer to the werewolf. You issue your final command.

Hurry to PAGE 8.

Marcie chases you all over the room, swatting.

"Stop!" you squeak. "I'm not a bat! I'm a human!"

But she can't hear your words. How can you get her to recognize you? You glance down at the cardboard letters on the floor and get an idea.

You fake her out with a quick twist and then swoop toward the letters. You grab the "H" and fly up to the top of a bookcase with it.

"Put that down!" Marcie shrieks.

You put it down all right. You lean it against a book, where she can see it. Then, flying as fast as you can, you snag a letter "E" and place that letter next to the "H."

Marcie still holds the flyswatter up, ready to hit you. But now she's staring at you curiously.

Quickly, you add the "L" and the "P" to the "H" and "E."

You've managed to spell "HELP" on top of the bookshelf. You hover near Marcie. If you could cross your webbed fingers, you would. Marcie gazes at the letters on the bookshelf. Then she stares at you. She glances back at the letters. "It was you!" she says finally. "It wasn't Darryl. You made the message!"

You feel like cheering. But all you can do is squeak. Quickly, you swoop back down for more letters.

Turn to PAGE 50.

Somehow, since you went to bed, your bathroom has grown to ten times its normal size.

Or you've shrunk.

I must be dreaming, you think. You climb up on the bathroom sink and stare into the mirror. The face gazing out at you from the mirror isn't your own.

It's the furry face of a small, hairy creature with a short nose, huge ears, and tiny white fangs.

It's the face of a bat!

You wink your right eye, and, to your horror, the bat in the mirror winks at the same time. The bat in the mirror is *you!*

"No!" you scream. It comes out as a tiny squeak.

This can't be real, you think. It's got to be a dream, right? You try to pinch yourself, but you can't work your bat fingers.

You continue to stare at your reflection, horrified. How could this have happened?

You think back over the last evening. You try to remember every detail. You hung out with your new friends at the Horror Club. There was a contest to find the scariest things. And then you remember something else — something that sends a chill down your furry little back!

What do you remember? Turn to PAGE 102.

"What is it?" you ask desperately. "What is the way out?"

The little man sighs. "First, you'll have to come work for me, as a snake charmer," he says. "Can you play the flute?"

"Well, uh, no," you reply.

"You'd better learn," the man warns you. "Otherwise, the snakes here will eat you in one gulp!"

He hands you the flute. You blow into it. The noise that comes out hurts your ears. The snake returns and angrily opens its mouth.

You try again. This time the note sounds better. The snake snaps its mouth shut.

"You'll need to practice ten hours a day," the little man tells you. "But that's only for three years. Because after three years, you will be allowed to return home. Now, if you'll excuse me, I'm going off to eat lunch."

As soon as he's gone, you start to put down the flute and leave. But the huge snake hisses violently at you. It opens its mouth threateningly.

With a sigh, you pick up the flute again. You always hated piano lessons, but this is ridiculous! You're sure that no kid ever had to worry about getting eaten if he didn't practice!

THE END

You wrench open the orange door, step forward, and plunge down. Down. Down. Cold air whooshes around you as you fall faster. And land with a *THUMP!*

You sit up slowly and examine yourself. You move your arms and legs. No broken bones. But where are you?

There's a sliver of bright light near your feet. You can reach out in the darkness and feel four walls around you. You're in some sort of closet! And it smells strangely familiar. Like old sweat socks!

You gaze behind you in the dim light. T-shirts, jeans, and jackets hang on a rod. Above the rod is one shelf filled with toys. Familiar toys.

With a shock you realize it's *your* closet — at home!

You open the closet door and step into your bedroom. Morning sunlight pours through the window.

"Time to get up!" you hear your mother call. "Come on, sleepyhead. It's Friday. Only one more day till the weekend."

Friday! Somehow you have been sent back to your own house on the morning *before* you joined the Horror Club! None of the scary things have happened to you — yet.

But they could. It's up to you. Are you brave enough to visit Bat Wing Hall again?

Turn to PAGE 1.

Nick is right. You'll have to go into the cage.

Still holding the witch's broom, you approach the werewolf. Connor and Debbie laugh, but you focus on the hairy beast. With each step you take, it growls louder. Then, suddenly, the creature whimpers. His ears flatten against his head.

He's afraid, you realize. But of what?

You reach for the cage door. The werewolf whines loudly.

The broom! It's scared of the witch's broom! You don't know why. And you don't care.

You hold the broom in front of you with confidence. You open the door and squeeze into the cage. The beast lunges at you!

Quickly, you thrust the broom at it. The werewolf backs off. But only a few paces.

"Nice going, wimp!" Connor taunts. "Only two minutes left!"

The werewolf drops to all fours. He snarls, sniffing at you and the broom. Now he reminds you of a very large dog.

Hey, you think, maybe the answer is to treat the werewolf like a dog. Command him the same way you command your own dog.

Or you could pretend to be a wolf. Maybe that way he will let you get close enough to pluck hairs.

Which do you try? If you try to command him, turn to PAGE 122.

If you pretend to be a wolf, turn to PAGE 101.

Nick and Debbie quickly leave your side and huddle together with the other kids. You can hear them arguing. Arguing about you.

Then one voice rises above the others. "But today is game day! You know what that means!"

"I don't," you suddenly call out. You're sick of standing there. You want to know what's going on.

It works. All six kids stop arguing.

The girl with the red hair steps toward you. "I'm Marcie," she tells you. "There are no stories tonight. We're playing games instead. But new members can't play. It's the rule."

"Can't you break the rules just this one time?" you ask.

"These aren't ordinary games," warns the boy with the large muscles. "These games are scary. Really scary."

"The scarier the better," you announce bravely. This starts another argument. Some kids want you to stay and play. Others want you to leave.

Debbie hurries over to your side. Through her mane of dark hair, she whispers, "Go home. Go home now!"

But at that moment, Marcie announces, "It's decided. You can stay and play games with us."

"Great!" you say, ignoring Debbie. "What are we playing?"

Learn about the games on PAGE 66.

CLANG! The werewolf crashes head-on into the side of the cage. He howls in frustration. His fangs snap at you.

You back up a step. You bite your lip as you stare at the hairy beast.

Familiar laughter fills the room as Nick, Debbie, and Connor slide down the basement's staircase bannister.

"What's the matter?" Nick taunts you. "Not having fun?"

"Only four minutes left," Connor reminds you, pointing at his small watch. "If you don't get three hairs from the werewolf by then, you'll turn into one of us!"

"But that's not so bad, is it?" Debbie says. "I mean, don't you think I'm beautiful?" She plucks a tarantula from her hair and wiggles it at you. You gaze at her hideous face and shudder. You'll do anything to avoid turning into a monster like her!

Cautiously, you step up to the cage. You stick your hand between the iron bars. Slowly, slowly you reach for the werewolf.

"WRROOWL!" The beast's jaws snap at your fingers, barely missing them. You pull your hand back, trembling.

"There's only one way to get the hairs," Nick says. "You'll have to go into the werewolf's cage."

Go to PAGE 127.

You've decided to make your friends move the club. You need to come up with some place better to meet than Bat Wing Hall. Then an idea comes to you. You know they won't be able to resist a challenge.

"I'm sorry I'm late," you tell them, entering the living room. "I was at the graveyard. I found a way cool place for us to meet. But it might be too scary for you guys."

"No way!" Martin protests.

"Are you sure?" you ask them. "Maybe we should wait and ask the other members?"

"Who needs them?" Martin declares. "Let's go for it!"

"Yeah," Marcie chimes in. "Let's check it out now. If it's spooky enough, it'll be the club's new home."

Great! That was easier than you thought. You lead your friends to the cemetery. The old gravestones poke out of the ground at odd angles. They're broken and covered with moss, and all their writing has crumbled away.

"Cool!" Marcie crows. "You were right. This is much scarier than Bat Wing Hall. Let's make this — " she stops suddenly and stares at the ground in horror.

You wonder what grabbed her attention. Then you see it! Breaking through the surface of the ground is a bony hand!

Turn to PAGE 63.

You slide open the door and lift yourself up into a moonlit room with a slanted ceiling. Old furniture and trunks of clothes are strewn everywhere.

Crouching, you make your way over to a little window. You peer out. And sigh. You are three stories up. You must be in the attic, you realize. There's no way you can jump out of the window. You'll never make it to the ground alive.

You shuffle back across the floor, trying to think of a plan. As you poke around in the junk, you spot a tall, clear box at the far end of the attic. There appears to be something black in it. And leaning against it is a broom.

Could that be the witch's broom — the one on the scavenger hunt list? You hurry over to investigate.

"Help me!" a shrill voice cries as you reach for the broom.

The voice is coming from the box! There's a woman trapped inside!

Her face is lined with deep wrinkles. Her long, knotted gray hair flows over a black dress.

"Wow!" You gasp.

The woman stares at you. Her green eyes seem to pierce through your flesh. "At last!" she wails. "I've been waiting two hundred years for you!"

Turn to PAGE 107.

"Leave me alone, kid!" you squeak. You crawl out of the drawer and swoop over to the letters. You've decided to spell out your name. That way Marcie will know the bat is really you.

You start searching through the pile of letters. You hear Darryl moving toward you. You search faster. Darryl's toddling closer. But he's so excited that he falls down. You've found the first letter of your first name. Quickly, you search for the other letters.

You've just finished finding all the letters in your name when Darryl reaches you. You look up to see him towering over you. He's about to lose his balance again. He reaches for a cabinet to steady himself.

"Be careful!" you squeak. "You're going to pull that — "

CRASH!

Whoops! Darryl pulled the cabinet over. Unfortunately, it was very heavy. Even more unfortunately, you were directly underneath it.

Too bad. Now you won't even get to be on TV — unless they come up with a show called "Flat Pet Tricks."

THE END

The next morning you wake up as a kid again. You're pretty sure you can avoid being toasted if you stay out of the sun as much as possible and really cover up. To be safe, you wear your hat, sunglasses, muffler, and gloves.

"Why are you dressed like that?" Marcie asks when you meet your friends at the mall. She and the others laugh.

"Maybe we were wrong about you," Martin teases. "Maybe you're too weird for the Horror Club."

"Why are you wearing all those clothes?" Marcie asks again.

You'd better rethink this. You'd hate to lose the only friends you have. "My mom," you say, rolling your eyes. "I'm getting a cold and this is what she did to me."

"My mom's the same way," Lara agrees sympathetically.

You'll have to wait for a better time to tell them the truth. "So what's the plan?" you ask.

"Let's check out the new science store," Lara suggests.

"I'd rather go to the movies," Martin says. "*Dracula* is about to start."

"Let's let the newest member of the Horror Club decide," Marcie says, turning to you.

It's up to you now. If you choose to check out the science store, turn to PAGE 73.

If you'd rather see Dracula, *go to PAGE 108.*

You've decided to wait for the monster's help.

"How do you like our library?" the blue head asks.

"It's very nice," you say. "Those are cool-looking monster books. But I *really* need to go back home."

"All in good time," the red head rumbles. "Can you read?"

"Well, of course I can," you answer. You wonder if the monster is going to write down directions for you.

"Great!" the red head cries. "We love being read to. Our librarian was a good reader, until she became a Swamp Thing snack. After you read our favorite stories to us, we'll show you how to go home."

"If you won't," the blue head adds, leering at you with its enormous yellow eye, "we'll eat you. Are you ready?"

You don't have much choice. But how hard could it be to read a couple of stories? The monster leads you into the next room.

"Which story should I read?" you ask.

"All of them," insists the blue head. The monster points to the shelves. You can see that they contain thousands of books. "The rest are in the basement," the red head adds.

Too bad — it looks as if you're going to be busy for a while. If you ever want to get home, you better learn to speed-read!

THE END

You have to break your fall! You reach out your arms and drag your fingers along the wall of the crevice. It slows you down a bit. Then the light begins to change, and you don't have to fight so hard to slow your descent. By the time you reach the bottom, you're almost floating. You land gently on a bed of moss.

You scan your new surroundings. You seem to be in a swamp. A swamp full of strange, twisted trees, and flitting insects. A smell of decay overwhelms you and mournful cries fill the air. You're overcome by a feeling of dread.

You want to get out of this creepy place — quick!

You run along a river bank, hoping it will lead somewhere. But before you have gone far, you come to a broken sign pointing in two directions. One part of the sign points across the river: TO THE CRYPT. The other part points to the path, but it is so old and weathered that it has no words left on it at all. Which way should you go?

Follow the path on PAGE 87.
Cross the river on PAGE 59.

"Please," you beg. "It's important. We've got to stop meeting in the mansion."

"No way," Martin says. "If you don't like it here, go form your own club."

"But — " you start to protest. But at that moment Professor Krupnik's ghostly voice fills the room. "YOU FAILED!" it moans. "NOW I MUST TAKE MATTERS INTO MY OWN HANDS!"

The room suddenly fills with smoke and bright flashes of light. Your friends start to scream.

"Wait — " you cry. But your voice comes out as a high-pitched squeak. In horror, you realize it's too late. You've turned back into a bat. You glance around to see three other bats flying around the living room in panic.

"Help!" Lara squeaks in her bat voice. "What's happened?"

"We've all been turned into bats," you say sadly.

Too bad! You made the wrong choice. But at least you'll have someone to hang around with.

THE END

Your bat's stomach insists moths are delicious. Following the sonar, you swoop into the tree and grab the insect in your jaws. Its body feels soft and powdery, and the bitter flavor makes you want to hurl. But you're starving. Gagging, you swallow. Then you zoom after another moth.

When you've finished your mothy meal, you fly straight for the graveyard and the Krupnik Crypt, landing on the top of the open door.

The door is bigger than you remembered. But then, you're a lot smaller. You drop to the ground and try pushing against it. It doesn't move. Even an inch. You fly into it, but all that happens is you bruise your wings.

What will you do? As a bat, you're too weak to close the door. When you're a human, you can't leave the house. Then you think of your Horror Club team. Maybe you can get them to help you.

But who should you ask first? Martin's the strongest, Lara's the friendliest, but Marcie seems the bravest.

Quick — decide who to visit and fly to their house!

Visit Martin on PAGE 36.
Or Lara on PAGE 118.
Or Marcie on PAGE 5.

About the Author

R.L. STINE is the author of over three dozen best-selling thrillers and mysteries for young people. Recent titles for teenagers include *I Saw You That Night!*, *Call Waiting*, *Halloween Night II*, *The Dead Girlfriend* and *The Baby-sitter IV*, all published by Scholastic. He is also the author of the *Fear Street* series.

Bob lives in New York City with his wife, Jane, and fifteen-year-old son, Matt.

GET
Goosebumps®
by R.L. Stine

❏ BAB45365-3	#1	Welcome to Dead House	$3.50
❏ BAB45369-6	#5	The Curse of the Mummy's Tomb	$3.50
❏ BAB49445-7	#10	The Ghost Next Door	$3.50
❏ BAB49450-3	#15	You Can't Scare Me!	$3.50
❏ BAB47742-0	#20	The Scarecrow Walks at Midnight	$3.50
❏ BAB48355-2	#25	Attack of the Mutant	$3.50
❏ BAB48350-1	#26	My Hairiest Adventure	$3.50
❏ BAB48351-X	#27	A Night in Terror Tower	$3.50
❏ BAB48352-8	#28	The Cuckoo Clock of Doom	$3.50
❏ BAB48347-1	#29	Monster Blood III	$3.50
❏ BAB48348-X	#30	It Came from Beneath the Sink	$3.50
❏ BAB48349-8	#31	The Night of the Living Dummy II	$3.50
❏ BAB48344-7	#32	The Barking Ghost	$3.50
❏ BAB48345-5	#33	The Horror at Camp Jellyjam	$3.50
❏ BAB48346-3	#34	Revenge of the Lawn Gnomes	$3.50
❏ BAB48340-4	#35	A Shocker on Shock Street	$3.50
❏ BAB56873-6	#36	The Haunted Mask II	$3.50
❏ BAB56874-4	#37	The Headless Ghost	$3.50

Scare me, thrill me, mail me GOOSEBUMPS Now!

Available wherever you buy books, or use this order form. Scholastic Inc., P.O. Box 7502, 2931 East McCarty Street, Jefferson City, MO 65102

Please send me the books I have checked above. I am enclosing $_____ (please add $2.00 to cover shipping and handling). Send check or money order — no cash or C.O.D.s please.

Name _____ Age _____

Address_____

City_____ State/Zip _____

Please allow four to six weeks for delivery. Offer good in the U.S. only. Sorry, mail orders are not available to residents of Canada. Prices subject to change.